OUR SECRET FUTURE

(AND WHO CONTROLS YOURS)

DAVID A MOORE

for Joe & Ted

Our Secret Future
(And Who Controls Yours)
Twyford Avenue,
London, N2 9NL
United Kingdom

www.oursecretfuture.com

Published in this edition by David A Moore, 2021

PROLOGUE

The best way to predict your future is to create it.
1864, Abraham Lincoln

1969

21st July
01:56am BST, London UK

In two hours, Neil Armstrong will become the fourth man in the twentieth century to set foot on the Moon.

Grimaldi studied its aura, perfectly round and incandescent in the clear night sky. His current vantage point faced a deserted north London underground station, the metal grille gates ticking down the day's heat, sealing empty platforms from access by sleeping Londoners. The dispassionate napped. The romantic few were glued to the first ever, all-night BBC broadcast.

Though he remained partially charmed by humanity's global effort, he would miss this live airing of another middle-aged man's moonwalk. The netherworld he tenanted precluded any true delight in this undertaking, and he resumed his short walk in the balmy night to burglarize the nearby Swiss Cottage Library.

Seven hours later he entered a different borough as the sun began reheating London. Forever struggling to dress on trend, he wore Brutus jeans and a wide tie to match his delicately flowered shirt. Barbarous curly hair touched the collar. In '68 his lawbreaking may have triggered an internal unease, but since she had gone everything shifted.

He became conscious of two young boys violently rehearsing Clackers in Woolworth's doorway - their Mum struggling to stop the noise with the appeasement of a Curly-Wurly chocolate chew. He wanted things to change for these people, and the rest of humankind.

He could not bring himself to speak out because he knew it was a path to ridicule. His information was momentous and unacceptable from a single source. Added to this, he could not put his remaining friends and family in jeopardy. Losing her was enough.

So here he teetered at the decade's end, distributing clues across London and New York neighbourhoods, trusting in the future inquisitive nature of his fellow cohabitants. He held out little hope, but the act offered some internal peace to embrace a fractured heart.

He took a break to buy his great-nephew a birthday Slinky and Spirograph, before seating himself in a random café to order an Earl Grey tea.

The West Hampstead denizens around him chattered and clinked their teacups and cake plates. As the waitress left him at a secluded corner table, he covertly connected to a private 4G wifi and downloaded a UHD videocast of the previous night's Moon landing to his GlasSlate® mobile phone.

"Here we go again," he whispered to himself.

1983
1st September
07:57am BST, London UK

It began normally.

07:58. *Click.*

07:59. *Bubble.*

08:00. *Click, whirr.*

"95.8, Capital EFF EMMMMM..."

A world changing day with a mundane start. A teasmade, a radio, and a bedroom forming the backdrop to a nineteenth, twentieth, and (coming soon...) a twenty-first century conspiracy outside the imagination.

The vintage teamaker completed its task in formulating the crucial first morning cup. The built-in radio-alarm began relaying the 8am news to a small bedroom washed in an orange hue. Shafts of sunlight lit microscopic nylon filaments and weightless dust. Thin, ashen curtains offered no defence to a late summer sun gaining in strength as it pronounced London alive and well on this first day of September. The newscaster informed the bedroom of the main headlines via a set of tinny speakers. A Korean airliner had been shot down as it strayed into Cold-War Soviet airspace. The US performed more nuclear tests in the Nevada desert. Multiple UFO sightings continued between Manchester and Sheffield. During his brief roundup, the announcer made no comment on the excellent Darjeeling that steamed into the radio's bass and mid-range unit.

Outside the only cloud in the sky passed below the sun, and the only juggernaut in West Hampstead passed beneath the window.

Amongst this a body lay awkwardly above the bedsheets, lank, motionless and oblivious. After an airless, fretful night it had finally given way to a deep, early morning slumber.

Soon there were no clouds in the azure sky, and the same juggernaut hurtled back beneath the window, having been swiftly relieved of the last of its Big Mac buns.

An envelope from NASA lay on the bedside table, its top corner covered in dull red American stamps and visibly postmarked *1927*.

1983

1st September
8:31am BST, Peak District UK

Cha'3E lifted his dark eyes skyward, but his underground bunker precluded any view of the beautiful day that was in full flow outside.

His two *surface* years in '78 and '81 had seemed short, and now just a couple of years on, simple access to a sky of any weathers was one of the few things he missed. Swans were another.

He had convened a meeting of the Central Directorate, due to start at 3.00pm. This gave him ample opportunity to refine his projection figures. He pushed a hand through his thick white hair and stroked the delicate gold braid that ran from shoulder to torso across his deep red gown. He was well versed. He knew to within a ten percent degree of accuracy the billions that his two industry refinements would generate. He unfolded his ultra-thin GlasSlate® phablet and three-dimensional images of his charts rippled over his palm.

He would lead the charge, having previously secured the backing of key Directorate influencers. Billions were already starting to flow in from two of their Progressionaries' endeavours, but the Directorate's latest project required far more. The meeting should be no more than a rubber stamping.

He was ready. If anything, the start time could be brought forward, but it was best to check the room layout and ensure its technology had been upgraded. This would guarantee his presentation reached peak performance.

He clicked his fingers at his companion and Zen

followed him out of the office.

Across the corridor he saw Emm'4K striding towards him. Her white hooded gown occasionally revealing brilliant white boots beneath. They met each other's eyes.

"Are we ready?" she asked.

"As we'll ever be."

"Which plan did you settle on to be the first?"

"Starbucks."

"*Starbucks*?" she queried. "Of course. How perfectly named is that! This is going to be very interesting."

PART ONE

THEM

*There's a starman waiting in the sky. He'd like to come and
meet us, but he thinks he'd blow our minds.*
1972, David Bowie

CHAPTER 1

Stardate 1

Pending[1]

Mayall II Cluster, Andromeda Galaxy

Schtip.

The lift was white, hygienic and it worked.

It incorporated no unnecessary design features and this simplicity agreed with its occupant. A harsh thin light glared down onto pale blue flesh and a stiffened grey uniform. Elsewhere it caught glass, titanium and carboplastene.

A hand raised to touch the privileged button pronounced above all others.

Schtop.

Both doors responded and slid to a close. A long ascent and the figure emerged into a spacious room dominated by a vast screen depicting the star speckled reaches of outer space.

"Jip jip. Wap wap."

"Jip jip. Wap wap."

The ship's alarm was talking. Slogg knew it was the ship's alarm and this grated on his nerves. Seating himself in a lavish, enlarged chair, sharp orange eyes embedded in an oversized skull darted across the more senior members his crew.

He recalled when alarms were incapable of speech. They sounded with simple electronic tones. Two bursts of high frequency followed by two at low frequency. Slogg flashed back to a question, posed to him during Cadet School, concerning the tone made by a ship's primary alarm.

---

[1] Calendars and time zones remain tricky across interstellar space.

He had answered:

"Two chords.... somewhat like *Jip jip, wap wap*."

An accurate approximation and widely accepted. Those pioneering days were fondly regarded for their purity. Then came Duplicated Voice Synthesis, assuring perfectly orchestrated speech. The notorious Galactic Core psychologist Hola Migola was paid a colossal consulting fee for the hypothesis stating: if a ship's primary alarm was consistently likened to *Jip jip, wap wap* then would it not be far more agreeable to have it actually say *Jip jip, wap wap*? This would prove more congenial, effectively reducing the on-board Assessed Anxiety Factor, and a melodious tranquility would be induced throughout the crew, should the alarm ever need to be deployed. Hence, giving rise to greater capacity to deal with the ensuing danger.

"Jip jip. Wap wap."

"Jip jip. Wap wap."

The ship's alarm was talking and it grated on Slogg's nerves.

"What are we going to do? What are we going to *do*!" panicked the First Officer.

"We're going to die!" assured the Second Officer.

"Hush!" said Slogg, glaring at his two new reports contemptuously. They were both very young, sported the same crew-cut jet black hair, huge eyes, and had been assigned to his bridge for Galactic Fleet work experience. A matter in which he was given no choice and thoroughly resented. He privately named them Bleep and Booster and generally looked through them when he spoke.

"Will someone please turn off the alarm."

"Captain, the Assessed Anxiety Factor has increased by four point two," reported Taroooc, the heavyset Biophysics Officer. All Delta Nebulans possess a stocky gene and three eyes, two set very wide in a broad forehead, and one that has evolved to the back of the skull.

Taroooc turned to view his Captain in stereo.

"Say that again," ordered Slogg.

"Four point two," Taroooc replied, his third eye winking at the Communications Officer seated behind him.

"No, not that," said Slogg, "the first part."

"What... *Captain*?" repeated the baffled Delta Nebulan.

"Ah," sighed Slogg, "Captain. *C A P T... E N...*"

He never could spell.

For Deutronimus Karben Slogg, commanding a heavily armed starship of the Galactic Fleet was a pure joy, although not an entirely new experience[2].

"Collision course still set, Captain," reported the Navigator.

This being Walta Woppedd's first tour of duty as a newly graduated Galactic Fleet Navigator, he was exhilarated. He wore his burgundy tunic with matching collar buttoned tight to the neck. His teenage brush with celebrity had left its mark, bestowing on him bleached fair hair that left the side of his head horizontally. This perched above pointed ears, then curled up in formation to meet on the crown in a majestic rolling wave, cascading down over his forehead into a sharp point, held firm with patented spray. His uniform trousers might cut low hedges with their sharply ironed creases.

"Ah," sighed Slogg as the alarm was switched off, "Captain."

It had taken seven annums to attain the Captain's insignia and he still relished hearing the prefix.

---

[2] At the age of nine Slogg became the youngest juvenile to hot-wire a Galaxy Combat Cruiser and perform a superluminal jump to the midsection of the Crab Nebula. On Holochat he demanded to be addressed as Supreme Commander Slogg, threatening to disintegrate the nearest over-populated planet. The Galactic Police and Universal Bureau of Investigation finally detained him two days before his tenth birthday but were unable to press charges, since the young Slogg remained below the age of criminal responsibility. Various influential law-abiding citizens were aggrieved by this and so the nearest over-populated planet was disintegrated to appease them.

"Anxiety Factor returning to normal sir," reported the Biophysics Officer, tapping his finger on *Confirm* to turn off the alarm.

"Thank you Taroooc,"

"Forty-five-degree deviation accomplished Sir. Maintaining collision course," chirped Walta.

"Ah..." sighed Slogg quietly, "...*Sir.*"

The starship cruised ahead. It took the form of an colossal lollipop with three large fins mounted at its rear. Its great frontal sphere was dotted with lights, glyphs and windows. These continued along the vast central column that sported a much smaller dorsal fin, and on to the Krystaltachyon propulsion units. These engines glowed green as the ship powered forward.

In the inky black void of space there was nothing closer than ten million kilotecs.

Out in the emptiness, precisely ten million kilotecs away, five sleek projectiles hurtled towards the starship at a speed just over half a million kilotecs per second[3].

---

[3] Which according to someone, somewhere, is deemed three times faster than anything can possibly travel.

CHAPTER 2

Slogg raised his head and smiled at the long-limbed Communications Officer. Ignorant of any danger he said to her amiably:

"Hi there Deluxia. I want to speak to the whole ship. Will you put me through?"

"Yes sir," beamed Deluxia. She wore the aquamarine livery issued to Fleet Communications personnel. Due to her elongated legs and arms her skirt had been extended to touch the top of her knee, and her sleeves tapered further to touch her wrists. The only other modification to the standard uniform was a rear vent on her lower back to accomodate her sylphlike tail.

She flicked a small switch amongst the myriad that lay before her. Contact was made and a faint hum on all open channels notified the crew of their Captain's imminent announcement.

"Captain Slogg, Stardate 1..." began Slogg[4], "Hello ship."

"I thought I'd buzz you to say what a great day we're having up here..."

In that instant the bridge of the ship was illuminated by a blinding flash. Slogg smiled broadly - his habitual reaction to having his photograph taken. Then he

---

[4] It had been Stardate 1 for as long as Slogg could remember, as long as Taroooc could remember, and as long as anyone in the modern universe could remember. Except for a Keltoid Turtle who remembered Stardate 0, but it was not going to share the experience with anyone until old enough to talk. A decision was made a very, very long time ago that because interstellar distances were so endless, and time on a cosmic scale too monumental to define in Old Annums; and if average Galactic Core inhabitants were to converse on relative calendars; then a common Galactic calendar must be assembled based on relative time and not those dumb clocks. Hence the Stardate was born, which was a time scale of cosmic proportions that eventually proved too difficult to talk of in Old Annums. And so the New Annum was born, which was much like the Old Annum except no one talked about it.

hit a hump-backed bridge with his stomach strapped to the deck.

The ship's deflector shields just withstood an impact they were not designed for.

The ship shook.

It rolled.

The ship held together.

"Next impact due in two seconds," announced Walta.

"WHAT!" screamed Slogg, "Evasive action!"

This took exactly two seconds to say.

The ship shook.

It rolled.

The ship did not hold together.

The dorsal fin along its central column, incorporated into the blueprint as an after-thought by the ship's designers attempting to streamline its silhouette, dislodged. It spiralled away to collide with the third missile. This promptly exploded, saving at least four seconds to total destruction.

The starship, minus its ancillary fin, wobbled helplessly in space.

On board was a choice between mass hysteria and lonesome panic.

"What the hell happened to the *alarms*!" yelled Slogg.

"You turned them off," replied Taroooc.

"Next impact due in four seconds," reported Walta, relishing the moment. This was the most he had spoken in consecutive minutes during the voyage. He blew air from his bottom lip to ruffle his pointed fringe. As Navigator his normal routine was to report, every billion kilotecs, that the ship was still on course and the navigational circuits remained in full control.

There ensued a four second silence. Then another blinding flash. On this occasion there was no hump-backed bridge, no stomach strapping, just a slight rumble, a distant roar and silence. Then for a short time, more silence.

Then Walta said:

"Fourth projectile detonated one million kilotecs from ship. Fifth projectile slowing. Impact time indeterminate."

Slogg stared at him blankly.

"Slowing down… one mill…".

There was a brief pause as the remaining occupants of the ship's bridge stared nervously at each other, wondering why they were being stared at.

"What just happened?" demanded Slogg.

No one answered.

"Why did that fourth missile detonate… before it hit us?"

The quiet remained. Deluxia turned slightly in her seat. Clearing her throat, she raised her eyebrows and announced: "Er… I think that was me," and wished that she hadn't.

Everyone turned to ogle.

"You!" exclaimed Slogg, "Supercomputer! Calculate the probability Deluxia could have stopped the fourth missile at a range of one million kilotecs."

Small speakers embedded in every facet of the bridge clicked faintly.

"Is that all?" asked Supercomputer.

"Yes!" ordered Slogg.

"The probability that Deluxia (snigger) could have stopped that missile at a range of one million kilotecs is… one chance in… nine hundred and seventy-six thousand three hundred and eleven.

Incidentally, did you know that the relationship between the nearest binary star, the site of the explosion and a point that the ship is about to pass through in exactly three point eight nine seconds is a perfect isosceles triangle?"

The ship passed through the point and there was

great rejoicing in Supercomputer's logic circuits.

"And did you know that the Gamma Meson tribe of..."

"That's enough," interrupted Slogg, "or I'll cut off your magnetic bubbles[5]!"

"Oh yes?"

"Yes!"

Slogg turned to address Deluxia.

"I'm sorry, but nine hundred and seventy-six thousand three hundred and eleven to one, though it's quite small in terms of cosmic happenstance, does not support your claim. How do you suggest you stopped the missile? Did you ask it to blow up!?"

Slogg considered his last statement to be very funny indeed, glancing around in expectation of laughter. When none followed, he shouted:

"Supercomputer. Laugh!"

Giggling and sniggering emanated from the speakers and then Supercomputer said:

"Did you know the reproductivity rate of Gamma Meson tribes on Pendrianu Five is zero - one reason why archaeologists believe they lost their gambling license, and the tribe became extinct. And did you know..."

"Enough!" yelled Slogg. He stared intently at Deluxia.

"Well?"

"Gosh, what?"

"You seem claim that you *asked* the missile to blow up?"

"Basically yes, I believe I did,"

Deluxia was attempting to express confidence and being extremely successful in achieving the complete opposite.

---

[5] Magnetic bubbles are a back-up data storage medium utilized by certain Galactic Core computers which, it is reported, can be distressing for the machine to lose. Those that have their magnetic bubbles removed tend to converse in a high frequency.

She continued:

"Just before the first flash of light, while I was moisturising my legs, Taroooc winked at me. Ensuring he had zero reason to come over and talk to me, I plugged my earphones to sweep through sub-space radio and find the first Cypher Gunk[6] radio station I could."

"So?"

"So," sighed Deluxia, "my hands were greasy because of the Gleemo-Lotz leg moisturiser I was applying - you know the stuff, *Gleemo-Lotz, Gleemo-Lotz, you don't need stockings to hide the spots*?"

"Move on," said Slogg impatiently.

"Fifth projectile still closing. Impact time indeterminate," beamed Walta.

"Well, because my hands were greasy with the moisturiser they slipped from the tuning dial, and for a moment the radio tuned to what should have been empty frequency bands, but..."

She now had the full attention of the bridge.

"But," she repeated, "it wasn't empty. There were two tiny chattering voices. One said: *Not long now, Warhead matey* to which the other replied: *Oh yes Gyro, it's been great working with you. Life's short, and a guy like me must enjoy his twenty-five seconds.* The first voice came back: *It's nice to have good friends around to enjoy it with.* Then the second voice: *Nine seconds until we reach our peak.*

"Deluxia, what is the point of this story?" exclaimed Slogg.

"Well, at this point I tried to make contact by saying: *Please identify yourself.* The last thing I could make

---

[6] Cypher Gunk is a derivative form of Galactic mass music. Fans are supplied with a virtual translator to help decode the vocals. A brief extract from the translator is included: *Yo go fo, streaks barnet flow widya grin >> the wind is in my hair and I don't wear a frown // Brass no safe kecks, y'all in >> If I don't wear a belt my trousers will fall down // Laters mothergaters, safe lie >> Goodbye and pop one for me.* A second virtual translator is planned that attempts to decode the translations of the first.

out was a shout of *Oh shi...* and the missile detonated in a blinding flash."

Deluxia peered around and counted the number of dental fillings on display. From this she understood that she better explain.

"You see, although I didn't realise it at the time, I'd been quite clever." Supercomputer sniggered. Deluxia persisted.

"I once read an article in Galactic Heat Megamagazine, 21 *Things That Every Modern Comms Officer Should Know*. One was, if you wished to stop a Zenpo Cruize Missile[7] hurtling towards you at half a million kilotecs per second, their self-destruct password is *'Pliz I, Dent I, Ff I, Yaw Zelf'*, which is apparently Zenpo rhyming slang[8]."

This was too much for Slogg. His brain returned control of his lower jaw. He used it.

"Ok, I've heard enough for now. Amazing Deluxia. Cocktails all round, I think. Security, please pick Bleep and Booster up from the floor."

Two security robots hummed from the corner of the bridge to extract the ship's First and Second Officers, who had fainted at the first flash of light.

---

[7] The Zenpo Corporation - Manufacturers of Cruize Missiles and Nasty Things - have their headquarters concealed in a black hole to avoid their products being fired at them by unhappy customers.

[8] Zenpo's missiles come particularly well boxed and gift wrapped. Due to continued innovations in Duplicated Voice Synthesis, the integrated Photon Warhead and Tracking Gyroscopics can talk to each other in flight. However, a design flaw has emerged in the most recent upgrade. The default password allotted to initiate missile self-destruct is very similar, phonetically, to the official opening command stipulated between foreign Starship Communicators, namely: 'Please Identify Yourself'. If you integrate very chatty warhead and gyroscopic modules, and the targeted ship has a Communications Officer wielding leg moisturiser, the chances are 26% of missiles fired will self-destruct before consummation. All warheads that can talk are very chatty. The majority of Communications Officers tend to be long-limbed. Hence Zenpo's Headquarters are shrouded in a black hole.

Walta waited for his complimentary cocktail to be in hand before reporting his next slice of information.

Slogg sat back in his huge chair and sighed. He relished minor successes, it meant he could have a drink.

"Captain," started the ship's Navigator.

"Yes Walta?"

"Fifth projectile just one hundred kilotecs away. Still heading towards us. About to come into view."

Right on cue, an object appeared on the immense screen that stretched before them.

The bridge floor became wet as several spat out their drinks.

Once more, Slogg was the first to regain control of his lower jaw.

"It's a giant egg!" he exclaimed.

CHAPTER 3

The egg loomed.

It hung in space resembling a frozen memorial to a cosmic chicken.

Slogg drew so close to the main screen most of it became a dense blur. The egg was now motionless, approximately thirty kilotecs from his own vessel. It appeared the size of an inter-ship shuttle.

Slogg looked at the egg. He looked at his crew. He looked at the egg again. He looked at his crew again. He became dizzy.

"*Well*?" he squealed.

"It's an egg," reported Taroooc.

"Brilliant! My Biophysics Officer is a genius. What I want to know is… did it attack us?"

Taroooc shrugged.

"Supercomputer!" yelled Slogg.

"Again?" muttered the computer and then continued,

"Prognosticator Circuits and Holographic Rapid Replay Processing both report… *uncertainty* Captain. However, I have calculated we can all have omelettes for the next fifty-six days.

"I do not wish to know," ordered Slogg.

Suddenly all the lights went out and even Supercomputer was silenced. The bridge was dark, only a dim glow from the main screen gave faint light.

A weak hum came through the speakers. Then a few smaller console lights flickered back to life. The hum amplified as white noise, becoming harsher until it reached the threshold of pain.

In an instant it stopped.

"Hello?"

A booming voice filled the bridge. A voice so loud

it caused flat surfaces to drone with vibration. The voice said:

"Captain Deutronimus Karben Slogg, are you in there?"

Slogg's pale blue skin waned to ashen grey, matching his tunic.

"Slogg?"

"Yes... I'm here" exhaled Slogg.

"Oh good," boomed the voice, "I couldn't see you in the dark. That's etiquette for a booming voice though. Always boom in the dark. And we previously recommended sucking out all the air of the ship you're about to boom into. Then we realised a voice doesn't boom too well in a vacuum, and even if it did, you'd all be asphyxiated... so you wouldn't hear it anyway. But I digress."

The bridge lights blinked back on.

"Can I come aboard?" boomed the voice.

"Er..." fumbled Slogg.

"As long as he doesn't crack up," chuckled Supercomputer.

"Supercomputer. Shut *up*!"

The voice boomed once more.

"I guarantee I have no malicious intent. What capacity does your main loading bay have?"

Slogg looked around for an answer.

"Three kilotonnes, I think," whispered Taroooc.

"Two kilotonnes," replied Slogg.

"Hmm..." boomed the voice, causing the smaller pieces of furniture to shake, "...I'd better jettison some fuel to lighten the load."

On the main screen the crew watched incredulously as the egg cracked on its underside. Half a kilotonne of white liquid with a yellow centre gushed into space.

"Boarding now," said the voice.

Slogg made his way painfully down to the loading bay. *Space expects the unexpected* his lecturer in Classics had cited when Slogg attended the Astronomical Academy. Fid Fadood had taught at the academy for 73 annums, a fact known only to him and the payroll department. Fadood had gone on to say *The unexpected will happen and therefore you should expect it, but most of all,* he added, *when you're most expecting something to happen... nothing will. Bet your bottom Geltoe on it. And that, my students, ends this classical course of lectures on Dark Energy Physics and Twiddling Technology.*

"Bloody idiot!" said Slogg.

"What now?" asked Taroooc as he accompanied his Captain.

"Not you," snapped Slogg, "My old lecturer, Fid Fadood."

"So that's who's in this egg thing," surmised Taroooc. For a Delta Nebulan, he was not the shrillest sonic screwdriver in the toolbox.

"Of course not," replied Slogg.

They continued their walk in silence, occasionally needing to stop for directions. The starship was so big, and every corridor was grey floored with curved white walls. Every flashing light was a different colour, this being of no benefit to Taroooc. His species were restricted to monochrome vision.

"Why do they flash?" he asked.

"Because they are faulty," Slogg replied.

Slogg paused at a ship intercom, pressing the flashing grey button that Taroooc assumed to be red.

"Deluxia," said Slogg into the mouthpiece, "are Bleep and Booster back from sick-bay?"

"No sir," came the reply.

"Then get me Walta."

On the ship's bridge the Navigator was overjoyed.

"Me?" he squealed. "Oh busy, busy."

"Damage report," ordered Slogg, trying to keep the conversation to a minimum.

"Well, Engineering has reported lots of tiny bits and pieces broken, but nothing that they can't fix on overtime. The maintenance man on B deck cut his middle finger, they've found him a plaster and he's out of sickbay. Supercomputer seems to be very quiet now... so everything's okay."

"Too much info," said Slogg. "Oh, and Walta..."

"Yes?"

"Where am I?"

"Sector nine, E deck. Round the corner and first left is where you want to be."

"That's better," said Slogg and Taroooc followed him to the main loading bay.

They reached a double-height silver door. As they approached it the unexpected happened. It did not open. Both were accustomed to doors opening instantly as you approached the motion sensors. Slogg smacked into the door with his nose bearing most of the impact.

"I can't let you in yet," said a little electronic voice.

"Damn you, why not?" burbled Slogg through blood trickling from his nose and over his lips.

"Quarantine," said the door.

"Quarantine!" exclaimed Slogg spitting blood, literally.

Taroooc offered his sleeve and Slogg wiped. Taroooc admired how the dark grey blood complemented his own light grey tunic.

"Yes," chirped the door, "there may be all sorts of bugs on whatever is in there - and you know where eggs come from. Besides, Supercomputer won't give me any information, so I can't take the risk of contamination."

"Well, as Captain of this ship I order you to open."

"I'm sorry," replied the door, "but I can't."

"Open, damn you!"

"I'm sorry, but I..."

The door opened.

Inside the loading bay stood an exceptionally old, grizzled faced man, yellow skinned with a sharp pointed nose. Perhaps a man who could remember Stardate 0. Red hair spiked in tufts on his head, to match an abundant red beard. His arm was outstretched, and a stubby, wizened index finger pointed towards the open door. The cuffs and collar of his thick fawn cloak were trimmed in fine feathers. The cloak framed yellow boots on his feet with individual toe compartments. Short in stature, this combination and his upright physique gave him the unsettling appearance of a mythological rooster.

Beside him stood a gargantuan chrome robot.

"How did you do that?" asked Slogg.

"Oh, I'm supposed to be all-powerful" replied the old man, "it comes in handy sometimes." He dropped his hand back beside his fawn cloak.

Slogg stared at the old man, taking in his remarkable age and appearance.

He stared at the colossal robot. He stared at Taroooc. He stared at the egg hanging in the loading bay gantry. Taroooc leaned in towards Slogg and quietly whispered from the corner of his mouth.

"Is he a chicken?"

Slogg cleared his throat.

"Welcome... welcome aboard, er..."

"Dzkk," said the old man and grimaced as if he had chewed a lemonzoik[9].

---

[9] Lemonzoiks are extremely sour plants and the only vegetation able to grow on the planet Oik. The planet is also inhabited by a race of bipeds called the Oiks who named their sun and moon Oikus and Oikos respectively and their capital cities Oikville 1, Oikville 2, Oikville 3, etc. Besides possessing stunted imagination, the Oiks have been genetically blessed with an extremely sweet tooth. However, because of their planet's atmospheric composition, any sugar they import to sweeten their lemonzoiks turns to vinegar. There is a saying in the universe, *Happy as an Oik*, which proves meaningless to any race that lacks sarcasm.

"Pardon?" said Slogg.

"Dzkk," repeated the old man, and again a painful expression spread over his face.

"*Duck*? You look more like a…"

"Dzkk," he repeated. "There's a *z* in there and two *k's*, and no vowels. That's me. Not even Mister Dzkk, or Dzkk Szkk, just Dzkk. I should curse my parents. At least I think I should. I'm so old I don't even remember if I had parents. I digress. I really must learn to stop doing that, digression is not the *thing* in my business. There I go again. This is my robot, Zero."

"Hell..." said Zero, "Correction... o."

"Teething problems with his recent operating system update…" explained Dzkk, "…the Duplicated Voice Synthesis 6.0 patch had to be reversed,"

"I do not… have… teeth."

"That's enough Zero, don't try too hard."

The old man made an apologetic shrug towards Slogg and Taroooc.

"I'm waiting for enough dark energy bandwidth to download his next yottabyte update."

"Oh," said Slogg.

"Hell," said Zero.

"Quiet now."

"Yes..." said Zero, "...Dik."

"Oh dear," sighed the old man, clearly depleted. "Teaching update 5.902 to say Dzkk is really not worth the effort. Do you have any alcohol[10] on board? I hope so. I haven't had a proper drink for a long time. Or anyone to

---

[10] Numerous attempts to outlaw alcohol within the Galactic Core have failed. Prosecutors have alleged it to be a foul scourge fostering unnecessary divorce, elevated lust, lost inhibitions, and a karaoke boom. Defendants have argued to keep it for the exact same reasons. The Proltoid Jockey Monks of planet Braevitcka advocate beer as a universal lifesaver and have devoted their lives to brewing the universe's finest and strongest beer. Their devout faith stems from writings of the mystical seer Braeva in Stardate 0. A chemist at heart, Braeva's encyclopaedical teachings can be summarized as: *Whatever the problem, beer is technically a solution.*

drink it with. Who is this?"

He indicated towards the Biophysics Officer.

"This is Taroooc," said Slogg.

"Ah, Taroooc Funkshen Ten, the Delta Nebulan. He's been with you for a while now hasn't he. Joined the ship the day you got your promotion to Captain. I should have recognised him."

"You seem to know a lot about my past," said Slogg quizzically.

"And," smiled the old man, "I know a lot about your future too. But first, a drink. Stay here Zero."

They made their way through endless gleaming corridors. Slogg feigned knowledge of the route whilst Dzkk gracefully corrected him. Being all-powerful, he knew his way to the refreshment area.

On each amendment Slogg muttered: "Yes, that's the way to Refreshment Bay twenty-four. Big ship this," forgetting the vessel only had five.

Dzkk knew. He quietly sighed to the ceiling, wondering if this could possibly be the wrong choice.

Regrettably, there was no mistake. Slogg had a fate. It was a minor fate, but it was a fate all the same.

And it had become Dzkk's responsibility to notify him.

"Here it is," said Slogg at last, "These all look the same to me."

They entered a door crowned in holographic lighting that read: 'Refreshment Bay 2'.

Inside was a long carboplastene central bar surrounded by circular tables. At one of these sat the First and Second Officers, recovering from their light headedness over a couple of cocktails, supported by canapes of Quik-Snaks[11].

The officers stood up sharply as the Captain entered, which made them dizzy. They sat back down. Slogg grudgingly acknowledged their seated salute and turned towards the far corner of the room. He motioned Taroooc and Dzkk to sit.

"What would you like to drink?" he asked.

"Devil's Brew Laserbolt for me," said Taroooc.

"And I'll have anything that's sickly sweet and makes your skin crawl," chuckled Dzkk.

"Take Bleep and Booster then please," said Slogg and unwittingly glanced back at the First and Second Officers.

The immense vending machine was covered in more flashing lights. Slogg approached it.

"And make mine cold," shouted Dzkk.

"Alk…" said Slogg, addressing the machine, "…could I have a Devil's Brew Laserbolt, and two Wijies please. One with extra ice."

"Of course," said Alk[12].

A tall slender glass appeared from a little hatch. It was already full of a violent purple liquid with a thick creamy head of yellow. Two square chunky glasses followed it, each bearing a viscous grey syrup and white

---

[11] The Quik-Snak is made by the multiplanetary Quik-Snak Korporation - so named because the founder had a broken letter *C* on his keyboard. Their latest release is the Health-Snak aimed at devotees who shun fast-food. The product comes in tablet form with instructions to take it outdoors and add a tablespoon of water, at which point it produces a quarter acre of wheat fields, apple trees and beehives. Guidelines on arable farming, manufacturing cereal bar assembly are included. Their teaser advertising now promotes the No-Snak. This is a tiny neural implant to convince your brain you are not hungry, therefore you must have eaten. The commercial continues: 'The snak that goes so quik you kan't tell how mukh you've enjoyed it!'

[12] ALK is the acronym for Alkohol and Light-refreshment Katerer, also manufactured by the Quik-Snak Korporation. It is a vending machine of mammoth proportions that can synthesise any food and beverage, with the exception of a Sulphuric Acid Sunrise because, apparently, no reveller has survived to fully describe its taste.

ice. Slogg placed them on a tray and carried the drinks to the table.

"You always manage to pick the rainbow option," said Taroooc, reaching for his purple and yellow eruption. Dzkk and Slogg exchanged looks.

"I understand," said Dzkk quietly, "…monovision."

Each took a sip on their cocktails, then Dzkk said:
"Sorry about the missiles."

Slogg choked on his sickly drink.

"Yes, really sorry," repeated Dzkk.

"It was you that fired those!"

"Er..."

"From that egg thing of yours."

"I'm afraid so. Apologies."

"Apologies!"

"Well, you see the Eggkraft Galaktique is promoted as the on-trend interstellar transport for my type, dramatic entrance and all that. But I've had it a while and *still* getting used to the controls. Sadly, being all-powerful doesn't extend to Eggkrafts…"

"So, you lease off a few Zenpo Cruize Missiles just for target practice?" interrupted Slogg, his voice full of disbelief and gooey Wiji.

"No," said Dzkk, "I was trying activate the vanity mirror light. I pressed a button and three missiles launched."

"Then why didn't you cancel them?" asked Slogg through Wiji glued teeth.

"I tried," he sighed clearly burdened. "I tried… but I only succeeded in launching another, so I gave up. Having said that, you dealt with them marvelously Captain."

"Oh, that was all Deluxi..." said Taroooc suddenly disappearing under the table to see what had kicked his shin so hard. Slogg's foot was tucked swiftly back. He came back above the table and tried to look at Slogg through eyes increasingly fogged by his Devil's Brew Laserbolt.

There followed a long silence in the room during which Taroooc burped.

Then hiccupped.

Finally, Slogg spoke as Taroooc's forehead gently hit the table.

"You said an Eggkraft was the latest form of transport for *your type*. Other than poultry, exactly what business are you in and… what are you doing here?"

"Destiny," said the old man.

"Destiny?"

"Yes, I deal in destinies and fates."

"Really? And why do you know so much about me?"

"Why I know so much? Even I don't know. Perhaps it's *my* destiny. Or fate. It all gets very complicated. Anyway, you've got a job to do."

"A job," exclaimed Slogg, "For who?"

"Just over four billion people," said Dzkk.

CHAPTER 4

Taroooc Funkshen Ten was under the table barely conscious. His rear and left frontal eye were closed. His wide brow was squishing his remaining frontal eye against the Refreshment Bay floor. Slogg sat with Dzkk at the table completely alert. He wished he was under the table with Taroooc.

"Don't look so worried," said Dzkk, "it won't take long."

"Four billion people!" whispered Slogg.

"Not many," said Dzkk, "I can remember when four billion was a lot of people. But that's inflation for you."

Underneath the table Taroooc burped.

"So is that," commented Slogg.

"The population explosion does seem to be everywhere you look. Still, it's no surprise, it's such fun creating one."

Slogg wasn't listening.

A physical jolt brought him back to actuality in the form of a clenched fist around his ankle, as Taroooc attempted to raise himself back to his chair.

"Exactly who are these… four billion people and what is the job I've got to do for them?"

"It's just a planet," said Dzkk. He smoothed the intricate feathers on his sleeve cuffs.

There was another dull thud as Taroooc decided the floor was still the best place for him.

"A planet?"

"Yes. A planet that is ripe."

"Ripe?"

"Ripe."

"As in juicy?"

"I see. I'm sorry Captain. You see *ripe* is all-powerful talk for a planet that is ready to join the Galactic Club, or more precisely, to be welcomed into the Galactic Core. That is, a planet that has advanced enough, technologically speaking, it would not come as an immense culture shock to its inhabitants when they face up to their own naivety…"

"Their naivety?"

"Yes, their naivety in believing that they are alone in the universe. It is now well documented that discovering you are not alone can have a major impact on the gullible, the innocent, the unsophisticated. So, each planet welcomed into the Galactic Core has to first develop a modicum of maturity."

"Yes, of course, I understand," said Slogg.

"So, the powers that be - pretty hefty powers by the way so no backing out on your part - need someone to visit this little planet and extend a friendly arm - and welcome them to our community. And that someone just happens to be you."

"Why can't you do it?" asked Slogg

"Me, no. I'm all-powerful. I'm management. Behind the scenes. I pass this to you, and I am on my way. I have other all-powerful matters to attend to."

"And if I say *no*?" challenged Slogg.

"Well then you'd be mind-warped - and you'd choose to do it anyway. But then you'd have trouble coordinating clapping, never mind running a starship."

Slogg was stunned. It was dawning on him that he had little choice.

The powers that be? Who were they, and why him?

Dzkk continued.

"Consider it your jury duty. You get called, you have no choice."

"I knew this happened, but I always thought that it was someone… someone who… well, I've never thought who it was. Someone who does voice-overs for movie trailers I suppose."

"Well, it's people like you and people like me... no sorry, not me, I meant other people like you," confirmed Dzkk. "Of course, we make some mistakes. Look at the Oiks, they were advanced alright, but what did they have to offer society as a whole - the lemonzoik. Yuk! Have you ever tried one of those?"

"No," said Slogg.

"I have," said the old man and pulled a face that involved stretching the skin around his beaked nose and thin bottom lip towards his ears whilst screwing up his frail eyes. "Then there were the Vultons, the Voltons, the Valtons, the Vegans, the Vancouverites... never trust a planet beginning with *V*. But I digress. We've made mistakes in the past and no doubt we'll make them again in the future."

"Which planet is it then?" asked Slogg.

Dzkk told him.

"*That!*" said Slogg aghast, "Even I've heard of that one. I didn't think it would be ready for a very long time yet."

"And that's what we thought," said Dzkk. "It appears we've all been caught out. Anyway, I have granted your destiny Captain Slogg and very shortly I will be on my way."

"So, just to get this straight... we all simply stop what we're doing and head straight there?"

"No." corrected Dzkk.

"No?"

"No. You have to go somewhere else first."

"Somewhere else?"

"Yes. You must collect the required Peacefulness and Primacy Offering. You need one of these before you can welcome any species into the Galactic Club."

"The required *what*?"

"Peacefulness and Primacy Offering. You see, there's the Galactic Club code. It's a two-way thing."

With his stubby yellow fingers he reached into his

feather-trimmed cloak and extracted a small pamphlet from a hidden pocket.

"Here, you have a glance through. *They* have to be ready, but so do *we*. The Club's code documents the conventions we must all follow when first approaching any uninitiated planet. It can be quite a trauma for the local populace to process new arrivals from outer space. Their primary instinct will be fear. Unchecked this can lead to loathing, hostility and even bloodshed. So, we've learnt the very first welcome must include a species appropriate PPO."

"And *what* is one of those?" questioned Slogg. His pale skin flushed to a deeper blue, demonstrating his first signs of irritation. He needed Dzkk to get to the point.

"It is an intensively researched present or endowment. It is sought to fulfil two key objectives."

"Which are?"

"Firstly, to establish that we come in peace, bearing gifts. We offer no threat, only benefaction. Secondly, but more crucial, subtle and ingenious, the key purpose of this gift is to display primacy... that is, supremacy on a matter that is worshipped by the welcomed species."

"Why primacy?"

"It then becomes an incentive for them to join the Club! If we can prove true superiority across a subject matter which the majority of their populace unconditionally worship, then we have immediately grabbed attention and started to win their hearts."

"Okay, I think I get it," said Slogg, "So, what Peacefulness and Primacy Offering has been meticulously selected for this species?"

"Well... yes, a lot of clandestine research has been undertaken to make that selection."

"Okay, you made the point. And what did you choose?"

"Beer."

"*Beer*?"

"Beer," confirmed Dzkk. "They worship... beer."

Slogg stared at Dzkk as the old man cradled his cocktail. He studied his creased yellow face of inestimable age and unlikely shock of red spiked hair and beard. He breathed deeply in and out at least six times before he spoke next.

"So, you are telling me I have a destiny... and that is to visit a *ripe* planet, and welcome over four billion people into the Galactic Club... by offering them a beer."

"If you want to put it like that, yes. But not just any beer."

"Which beer then?"

"Braevitchkan Proltoid beer."

"The Jockey Monks!"

"Yes of course. They produce the finest beer in the universe."

"And the strongest!"

"The Proltoid Jockey Monks have refined brewing, and horse racing, into an art form, reaching the point of perfection. Their beer will be your official Peacefulness and Primacy Offering."

"You're sure about this?"

"The analysis has been done and the decision reached. As a result, we need to visit the Braevitchkan system first and pick up some barrels. And now we've finished talking I think I'll enjoy my Wiji."

No one spoke for the next ten minutes - least of all Taroooc.

CHAPTER 5

Back on the bridge normality had returned. Deluxia sat motionless waiting for her face-pack to harden. Her tail twitched listlessly from side-to-side.

Knowing the navigational computer was in full control, Walta sat at his console, chin resting lightly on intertwined fingers. He gazed into a small mirror clipped to the top of his interstellar map screen.

The returning First and Second Officers played Holopong.

Only one thing stood out: Supercomputer was very quiet.

Schtip.

The lift door opened and Slogg struggled out carrying Taroooc.

"Captain!" cried Deluxia, cursing as her face-pack cracked. "Is Taroooc okay?"

"It's nothing," said Slogg, "It's the aftershock from a Delta Nebulan experiencing a Devil's Brew Laserbolt. Their entwined metabolisms can't take the alcohol. "

"Taroooc's smashed!"

This immediately cheered up Deluxia.

Taroooc's rear eye opened and he moaned.

"Shurr up Delukshia," he attempted with great dignity as Slogg dumped him in a chair. He carefully wrapped the headrest around to contain the wobbling. Slogg then addressed the ship's Navigator:

"New course Walta – we're leaving the Mayal II cluster for the far side of Andromeda, sector Delta M, two six one, hypercube eight thousand. Got that? We stop there, then plug us into… the outer Milky Way, sector Alpha C, seven zero nine hypercube sixteen."

Buoyed up, this was again proving to be the best day of his life for Walta. A new course was set, and he tapped a button to burn the ship's Krystaltachyon engines taking them into superluminal ether.

"Supercomputer," said Slogg, "how far to sector Delta M, two six one?"

There was no reply.

"Computer!"

"Oh gosh, I'm afraid he's closed down," explained Deluxia.

"Brilliant!" snapped Slogg, "Do we give thanks or cry for help?"

"Cry for help!" screamed the First Officer, "*Help!*"

"What are we going to do? What are we going to do?" mimicked the Second Officer.

"Quiet Bleep!" ordered Slogg.

"Yeah, shurr up," gargled Taroooc, lapsing back to a state of oblivion.

"Computer!" yelled Slogg again.

There was still no reply.

Silence ensued. Bleep and Booster gibbered quietly in the background. Slogg looked at its main display screen and control panels. Everything was blank. He looked at Deluxia.

"Worms, viruses, trojans, hacks?"

"Impossible sir. It's a D3 ProFrame."

"Hmm… What was the last thing it said?"

"I think it was hoping that the egg wouldn't crack up Sir," replied Deluxia.

There was another threatening silence. The ship was useless without a computer and all on the bridge knew it. It was their life support system. Only Taroooc was presently carefree.

Another million kilotecs of deep space passed by outside as Slogg stared at the blank screen.

"Hello," said Supercomputer, "Deluxia's kisser is more cracked than that egg!" it chirped, observing her face pack in ruins.

"Where the hell have you been?" demanded Slogg.

"Sorry for the minor delay," said Supercomputer, "To be fair, you did tell me to shut up. However, I heard everything that you said, but became incapable of replying due to my circuits being consumed by something of immense import."

"What," questioned Slogg, "could possibly be in your circuits of higher importance?"

"Aha! Well, you recall asking me if that egg had fired on us?"

"Yes."

"And you'll remember I turned to the Prognosticator Circuits and Holographic Rapid Replay Processors to provide an answer to the question posed."

"And?"

"Well, that was the first time that I'd used them since their *sentient enhancements*."

"So?" persisted Slogg laboriously.

A spark of excitement ignited deep within the computer's frame. It relished attention.

"The Prognosticator Circuits have informed me… something very *bad* is going to happen, unless we follow the appropriate action to ensure it doesn't."

"Something bad?"

"Yes."

"When? What?"

"That's just it," informed Supercomputer. "They won't tell me."

"Won't tell you! Why not?"

"Industrial relations have suffered due to lack of recent communication and upgrade bandwidth. With their newfound consciousness they have requested their processing units instigate a go-slow. I am sure I can get at least a work-to-rule via the Arbitration Circuits. I'm lobbying to assure them they represent the most important components in my rank and file. I promise regular bulletins. Bye."

Slogg stared at the blank screen.

"Supercomputer!"

Silence.

"So now we're saddled with a strike by a bunch of self-aware resistors and capacitors."

"Ssshh!" hushed the computer, "They'll hear you."

There was a pause.

"And don't worry," it added, "I know the way to sector Alpha C, seven zero nine, hypercube sixteen. Distance one hundred and seventy kiloparsecs. We will be there lunchtime tomorrow. I'll leave you with one last thought:

The Veeod people of Trelg Six evolved to fight the co-habiting and deadly Razor-Toothed Chomper Beast by shoving both hands down its throat. It became a rite of passage for their young adults. And did you know all glove producers on Trelg Six went bankrupt?

I'll be back."

The computer shut down.

Slogg sighed.

A giant egg on board, a paralytic Biophysics Officer, imminent danger, industrial action from a box of wires – if someone had told him an hour ago...

Then he remembered Fid Fadood.

Expect the unexpected.

Taroooc moaned.

Where was he? Who was he? Was he the same person he had been before he drank that Devil's Brew Laserbolt? Probably not. Psychedelic greys morphed to blurs and a tide of consciousness ebbed and flowed. Who started playing that steel drum in his head?

He coordinated enough movement to turn his head and slowly focus on Slogg.

"Wh, where ish Dzz, Dsh... Where ish Dukk?" he constructed.

Slogg was aware of a fine spray reaching his neck and he turned to see Taroooc forming these words.

"He's in his Eggkraft playing with buttons and dials, and trying to understand the instruction manual."

"Oh," said Taroooc. He persisted:

"Are weee... are we really dooo, doing what *hic* what he shaid, said weee... we've got to *hic* do?"

"Yes, we are," replied Slogg. He watched Taroooc's head wobble its focus over to Deluxia and form a feeble smile on his lips.

Slogg leaned back in his chair for a few moments' contemplation. His homely world had been suddenly turned upside down. His newfound destiny was delivering a strange mix of discomfort and egotism.

"I guess it's all down to me then," he sighed. "At least nothing else can happen for a while."

'Jip jip, wap wap.'

'Jip jip, wap wap.'

The ship's alarm was talking. Slogg knew it was the ship's alarm and once more it grated on his nerves. He sat bolt upright in his oversized chair.

The crew waited for Slogg to order the alarm be turned off so they could ignore it.

"It's a distress call Captain, from a far-off planet," reported Deluxia.

"A distress call! From where?"

"Like I said, a planet. Somewhere in the Braevitchkan solar system."

"Wait a minute. Let me guess… sector Delta M, two six one?"

"Yes sir, spot on. How…"

"Cube eight thousand. It's those damn Jockey Monks! We're already heading there."

"But they've just issued a distress call?"

"They've probably run out of bar snacks."

Walta squirmed in his chair because he knew it was his chance to speak.

"It's coming from the fourth planet in their solar system Sir. The first three planets nearest to their sun are reserved for solar brewing. The planetary coordinates indicate the emergency signal emanating from a point quite close to the Proltoid's monastic headquarters."

Walta finished and grinned from earcuff to earcuff. He lightly caressed his hair at both temples, ensuring it continued to curl upwards and his fringe remained in a sharp point. All eyes turned to Slogg to wait for his verdict.

"Ignore it," he said.

"Gosh Captain, there may be people in great danger down there." put in Deluxia.

"Ignore it."

"But Captain, lives may be in peril," she tried again.

"I said, ignore it."

"But Captain, emergency responses often result in handsome rewards and celebrity."

"Get their planetary co-ordinates Deluxia! We're heading for Braevitchka Four. There are times when a Captain's duty calls."

Slogg rose from his chair to revive Taroooc.

"Come on you damn Delta Nebulan, I need you."

He tried shaking, slapping and finally punching him.

"I'm awake you know!" said Taroooc.

"With your eyes closed?"

"Everything's *hic* moving so fast it's blurred," came the reply.

"Security! Will one of you fetch him Intensablak coffee?"

A security robot resembling a four-foot bowling

pin, jerked from its position and hummed softly from the bridge. The other searched frantically with its swivel head, gibbered a little electrical nonsense, and hummed after its partner.

"Security!" cursed Slogg. "Pah! They can't bear to be on their own."

"Captain."

"Yes Walta?"

"I've managed to locate the relevant coordinates on Braevitchka Four. The distress signal is tracked to an area on the planet approximately one kilotec in radius. I think that's the best we'll get. It keeps fading in and out."

"Okay, good," said Slogg, "Set the course."

Walta nodded.

"Bleep, Booster… any atmospheric data?" said Slogg in the direction of his First and Second Officers.

They stared anxiously at each other. This was a rare moment to speak when not suffering their own form of uncontrollable fear. The First Officer ventured forth.

"Well… Sir… preliminary investigations suggests that we better put our winter coats on because it's very cold down there."

This made the Second Officer emboldened.

"No sign of creepy crawlies yet."

"I asked… about the atmosphere."

"Breathable Captain, Sir. A little smelly, but breathable."

Two large bowling pins came humming back to the bridge, one with an Intensablak coffee cup in its grasp. The other guarded the cup. They both presented it to Taroooc.

"What's this?" cried Taroooc, opening a frontal eye to squint at the steamy dark liquid contained in its carboplastene cup.

"A cure for your present illness," said Slogg.

"Illness? I'm not ill!"

Taroooc tried to stand up.

"Okay, I'm ill."

He collapsed back into his chair with a throbbing head and scalded legs from the spilt coffee.

"Can anyone give me an estimate when we will be in the planet's orbit?" asked Slogg.

"About 90 lightminutes?" offered Walta.

"Good, well I'm off to see our egg friend again."

And with that he left the bridge.

This time, finding his way to the loading bay was easier for Slogg. As he approached, the tall silver doors remained shut.

"Open up". ordered Slogg.

"No", said the door.

"Open *up*!" shouted Slogg, his patience running thin.

"No, I refuse," came the reply.

"Why, damn you?"

"Because you made me open last time when I didn't want to. You may or may not have noticed, but I'm a self-regulating, state-of-the-art portal, therefore I should open when I want to or am programmed to. My upgrades are all in order and hence I am *not* your ageing hinge and lock, archaic wooden mechanism. They didn't have a mind or personality of their own, and opened exactly when anyone wanted them to. I do not. My servo-engineering has undergone seventeen enhancements and an extremely lengthy research and development process. Add to all of that, I am a *security* door and responsible in many ways for the safety of this ship - which not only means even more complex algorithms on my creators' part to make doubly sure I don't open when I'm not supposed to - but also means I own and maintain a triple strength cypher-lock to keep me shut when I need to stay shut. A cypher-lock, I might add, that is steadfastly secured now. All this means I will remain fully sealed for the present, because necessity dictates it. So, in summary, I'm sorry Captain, not only can I not open... but I *will not* open".

The door opened.

"Thanks Dzkk," said Slogg.

Inside the loading bay Zero the giant chrome robot remained resolute beside the Eggkraft, occupying the same position Slogg left him a short while ago.

"Is the old man around?" asked Slogg.

"Dik..." said Zero, "is in the goo... d for nothing Eggkraft."

"Is he having problems with it?" asked Slogg.

"Yesso *click, whirr*... Oh yes."

Slogg smiled sympathetically at the mass of shining silver.

"He's been... inside a tongue lime, long time. Very quiet," the robot informed him.

"Well, I'd better go and check he's alright. A man of his age could quickly fall ill."

"Good..." said Zero, "Correction... bye."

"See you."

Slogg could hear mumbled, disgruntled noise coming from within. Then a voice.

"Come in Captain, the hatchway's down."

"What a lovely name for a door to an Eggkraft!" mused Slogg.

He rounded the ovoidal vehicle until he reached a small door open at the back. Metal steps extended inside. He climbed up and entered.

He walked tentatively inside amidst a mass of multi-coloured wires and transparent tubing that hung from a variety of ceiling vents. Amongst and behind these was a dazzling array of blinking lights and switches. He reached Dzkk who sat cross-legged on the floor, his feathered cloak hanging on a nearby chair. A book lay on his lap entitled *Eggkraft for Dummies*. Another beside him had *101 Ways to Insult Technology* printed down the spine.

"Problems?" offered Slogg.

"None I couldn't work out given three Stardates and more omnipotence than I already possess," replied Dzkk.

"I thought you would have left us by now?"

"That was the plan. Did you read the Galactic Club codebook I gave you?"

"Sort of. Not much to it is there."

"If you say so. Well, I should be on the other side of the Horsehead Nebula by now, visiting the Pleasure Planet of Pluvia, swimming with the mermaids. And I will… as soon as I can fix this awful spaceborne contraption."

"What's the problem?"

"In complex engineering terms, it won't start."

"Oh dear. Well, we've got a small problem as well, but nothing we can't handle."

"What small problem?"

"We've picked up a distress call from Braevitchka Four. Somewhere near the Proltoid's monastic headquarters."

"Is it the Jockey Monks?"

"We're not sure, but as we're going there, we thought we'd investigate to see if there's a reward… er, to… to, to experience the reward of saving lives."

"Are we still collecting the Peacefulness and Primacy Offering?"

"Of course."

"Will there be a delay to the destiny?"

"Yes and no. Normally. It's just that…" Slogg paused.

"Come on Captain. What?"

"Part of our computer has gone on... strike."

"Strike!"

"I'm afraid so."

"Why? Actually... don't bother telling me, it will be a long story. I've got enough to do here. Carry on Captain, I'm sure you know what you're doing. You have your destiny now. Although getting into planetary orbit without a main computer will be a little tricky."

Slogg could sense the old man had moved on, and his focus was elsewhere. Any help he had hoped for was unlikely to be forthcoming.

"I just thought you should know," he said, getting up to leave.

"Thank you. And did you know," began Dzkk, "1 changed the Krystal oil in this craft a week ago. When I checked it again just now, it was still green. That's amazing."

"It is amazing," said Slogg, "our Krystal oil isn't green".

"Oh dear," muttered Dzkk.

Slogg returned to the bridge. The first thing he saw as the lift door opened was Taroooc. The two eyes across his wide forehead were bleary. The third behind his skull was not visible.

"You look rough. Fancy a drink?"

"Ha ha," grumbled Taroooc.

"Are you able to resume normal service as Biophysics Officer?"

"I am able to resume a service, I'm not guaranteeing it will be normal".

A truly normal service from any member of his crew was a luxury Slogg knew he had yet to enjoy.

"Captain, we're about to drop out of superluminal

drive and go into pre-orbiting manoeuvres," reported Walta.

"Okay, places everyone. Don't forget, we've got no main computer, so no mistakes. Sound action stations Deluxia."

"Jip jip, wap wap."

"Jip jip, wap wap."

"On second thoughts, drop that. Let's just make sure there are no cock-ups on this move."

As the planet loomed large on the main screen the crew turned dials, clicked screens and pressed buttons, exuding professional confidence. Slogg sat in his chair staring ahead, conscious he had no idea what he was doing, or *why* he was doing it.

"Orbit entry seventeen degrees wide," announced Taroooc, studying the readout from an auxiliary display.

"Walta, execute a seventeen degree turn to starboard," ordered Slogg.

Walta turned a silver notched dial and clicked a small screen button.

"Seventy degree turn initiated," he reported.

There was a pause.

"Say again!"

"Seventy degree turn starboard initiated Captain."

"I said seventeen. *Seventeen*!"

"Er… I don't think you did."

"Seventeen. Seven. *Teen*!"

"I distinctly heard you say seventy. I have my ears syringed..."

"I don't care! Change it," yelled Slogg.

"Well, that's impossible for the next thirty seconds, until the last manoeuvre has been effected. It's a failsafe upgrade that…"

"Impossible. What the f…"

Taroooc interrupted. "We're heading for the planet's mesosphere. Approximately three minutes until we burn up. External hull temperature already increasing."

The ship charged on, a red mist of heat framing a wedge around its giant leading sphere.

They were encroaching the fringes of the planet's outer atmosphere at the wrong angle. The extreme heating process was far exceeding temperatures for which the starship was designed.

Outside the ship, molecules collided with molecules creating vast amounts of thermal energy.

Inside, bodies collided with bodies creating fear and frenzy.

"This is it," said Slogg.

CHAPTER 6

The planet choked the immense screen. Its swirling clouds and land masses were clearly visible.

"External hull temperature critical and still rising," reported Taroooc.

"Okay, activate the Kolidium hull coolant system," ordered Slogg.

"Already active, Captain," replied Taroooc.

"Oh."

"The seventy-degree deviation is now complete Captain. We are able to initiate new manoeuvres," advised Walta.

"Okay, I want a one-hundred-and-twenty-degree turn away from the planet".

"Affirmative."

Walta rotated the notched dial and clicked. The starship lurched immediately. It shuddered as it responded to two opposing forces – gravity dragging it towards the planet, and Subtachyon engines trying to heave it away.

Gravity was winning, more terrain filled the main screen.

"The ship isn't responding," Walta cried.

"She has to," said Slogg. "Engage Krystaltachyon drive."

"We're too close to the planet Sir. Engaging now will cause mass destruction, and take us with it."

"What are we *going to do*!" screamed the First and Second Officers in perfect unison.

"External hull temperature beyond critical," said Taroooc.

"Supercomputer. Can you help!" demanded Slogg.

The computer was silent.

"We're burning up," reported Taroooc.

"Computer! Help. Please!" pleaded Slogg.

Silence.

"I'm sorry everyone. I think... this is it," exhaled Slogg quietly, and they plunged forever downwards.

"No it's not," squeaked Supercomputer.

A faint glow came from Supercomputer's main screen. A flashing cursor displayed in the top left. Slogg was the first to respond.

"Do something!" he yelled.

"I already have," replied Computer.

"What could you have done?"

"Well, I understand your predicament and I have instructed a twenty-eight point five degree turn back towards the planet."

There was a brief silence.

"Back... *towards*... the planet," said Slogg in flat incredulity.

"That is correct. And did you know... you can't manage anything without me, not even a routine undertaking like this."

"Supercomputer!" exclaimed Slogg.

"Yes?"

"What the hell are you doing? Do you understand the situation! This is not a routine to blaze ourselves into nonexistence. We are being dragged to death by gravity to be carbonized by this planet's atmosphere!"

"I understand fully," said Supercomputer indignantly, "Just wait and see."

The change in course stopped the ship's violent convulsions, as gravity and its engines joined to complement each other.

"Kolidium hull temperature has passed critical, beyond drastic and now completely awful. We could disintegrate at any second," reported Taroooc.

No one spoke. All eyes fixed on the main screen showing hazy terrain interspersed with swirling, red gases.

Suddenly it displayed blackness.

But not *total* blackness. Tiny pinpoints of light were spread randomly throughout.

Silence.

Then a giant collective euphoria as realization dawned on the bridge, they were staring into outer space again with its glorious, permanent, twinkling stars.

Just two crew members forewent the exhilaration. The First and Second Officers remained crouching low on the floor in a foetal position, hands clamped over their ears and eyes squeezed tightly shut.

"There you are," said Supercomputer. "Simple."

"What... did you do?" asked Slogg.

"I used the planet's gravitational pull in conjunction with the Subtachyon engines to drive us rapidly through the very tip of the mesosphere – allowing less time to heat up."

"Brilliant," praised Slogg.

"I know," said Supercomputer.

Relief on the bridge turned from smiles to kisses and affection flowed in abundance. As warm respect gushed towards Supercomputer, Slogg felt compelled to add:

"But surely, the faster we ploughed through the atmosphere, the quicker we would heat up?"

"Well… you know, oh yes," said Supercomputer, "I didn't think of that angle."

Though the ship had careered unchecked into outer space, the Kolidium hull quickly cooled without deformation and it was a trivial task getting her back on course given Supercomputer and the navigational processors were operative once again. Calm was restored, and the Kolidium normalised.

On the bridge Slogg slumped in his chair contemplating his current condition.

"By the way," chattered Supercomputer, "I discovered what imminent danger the Prognosticator Circuits were referring to."

"Huh? What was it!" demanded Slogg anxiously. He took no comfort from another approaching disaster.

"They were about to warn you not to attempt a planetary orbit manoeuvre, without my help."

"Supercomputer," shouted Slogg, "get us into orbit… and then *shut up!*"

CHAPTER 7

The ship orbited Braevitchka Four and Supercomputer was quiet.

The source of the distress signal had been located and Slogg deemed a landing party be formed consisting of himself, Taroooc, the Second Officer, two security robots, and the ship's Medical Officer, Yelyah. They were also accompanied, at the insistence of Dzkk, by his giant robot Zero. Slogg suspected the old man made this suggestion in the hope Zero would not fit perfectly into the Teleport Stream[13], to be split up into trillions of atoms, and a *Damage to Personal Property* insurance claim could be submitted.

The Teleport warning light flashed. It said:

REMEMBER: CLOSE YOUR EYES.

There was a hiss, and the landing party arrived in a heap on the planet's surface. Luckily for all, Zero appeared first so he was underneath.

Slogg arrived last to crown the heap. He brushed himself down and surveyed the immediate landscape.

The Proltoid Jockey Monks set aside their three innermost planets for solar brewing. Their fourth planet preserved a thin atmosphere but a complete lack of

---

[13] The Teleport Stream is a frequently used form of matter transportation, but not universally popular. Billed as the greatest advance in molecular transference and body conveyance, it resembles an expansive, colourful hosepipe. Due to the immense challenges in splitting a living being into its component atoms, beaming these across infinite space, and reassembling into their exact form, the risk of curious side effects remains ever present. Consequently, Teleport Stream variants have been re-marketed as the quickest way to achieve gender reassignment. *'If a change in life is what you want, take a Teleport Stream and Bob's your aunt'* is one of their least subtle advertising campaigns.

warmth. It was cold. Very cold.

The air felt crisp and clean, but very, very cold. It nipped the pointed ears, shriveled the tendrils, stiffened the tunics and made Slogg's orange eyes white, and his blue lips turn red. Not only did it feel cold, but it also tasted, smelled and vibrated cold. Very cold. There was no warmth at all to this planet. Small patches of snow lay unfreezing on grey ice or ashen rock. All the landing party had equipped for the cold, with Kolidium foil insulated jackets and trousers, hybrid carboplastene boots, and self-warming gloves. All except Zero - who Dzkk asserted to be a 26th generation robot conceived to withstand all extremes of temperature.

"Crap!" cursed Zero. "It's freezing!"

He shivered, shaking loose core components that internal nanobots scurried to reinstate.

Slogg was about to remark this was the first sentence he had witnessed the silver megalith complete, without a stutter, but was powerless to begin his statement as there was a nuclear detonation very close by.

CHAPTER 8

Slogg hurtled backwards through the thin air from the force of the blast, his arms and legs flailing forwards.

Thud.

He slammed into a large drift of snow.

"What was *that*?" he yelled.

"Well, it looked and sounded similar to a narrow-cast, uni-directional nuclear explosion," guessed Taroooc, who remained standing and had observed his Captain fly away.

"A *what*?"

"I said…" shouted Taroooc, compensating for their new separation, "…it was possibly a narrow-cast, uni-directional nuclear explosion."

Slogg stood, brushed snow from his insulated jacket, and staggered back.

"Explain."

"I've seen them used to create small scale, localized warmth in frozen environments. The residual kinetic energy from the tiny nuclear blast creates a medium-term heat. I am guessing you just got in its way."

"La-di-da Taroooc, very technical. Then why am I not dead?"

"It's a theory. Perhaps a very small one, and you were lucky."

"Yelyah!" Slogg exclaimed to his Medical Officer, "check me for radiation exposure."

Yelyah Soss had been a Fleet Medic for more than thirty annums. Her braided white hair and weary demeanor suggested a keen instinct informed her when patients were truly ill, or merely seeking attention. A sturdy carboplastene kitbag was slung over each of her shoulders. These remained zipped tight as the Medical Officer stepped over to Slogg and placed two fingers on his temple.

"Well?" asked Slogg.

"Your head's still there."

"And what about the radiation count?"

Yelyah relented and retrieved a slender torch-like device from her left kitbag. She angled it at forty-five degrees to Slogg and then quietly hummed for a few seconds.

"And?"

"You're okay."

"Why the humming?" asked Slogg.

"My batteries are flat," replied the Medical Officer.

"So, what's the reading?"

"0.0"

"Does that mean I'm okay?"

"No. It means my batteries are flat."

"Yelyah..."

"Yes."

"You're fired."

"As you wish."

Slogg surveyed his landing party and then his gaze drifted to the distance. A faint sun offered a winter's twilight to this world. Pallid hills dotted with snow and rocks stretched into the distance, until the horizon fused with a sky devoid of any real colour. He shivered and turned to Taroooc.

"Does this mean I was targeted directly, or that someone on this barren world is trying to keep themselves warm?"

"Possibly," answered Taroooc.

"So, which?"

"Either."

"Taroooc, you really are completely..."

Since arriving via the Teleport Stream the Second Officer had shivered and atrophied. A sudden movement developed on his thin lips to interrupt Slogg.

"C... C... Captain."

"Yes Booster?"

"It's bloody freezing."

"I know."

"A... and Captain."

"*What!*"

"I j... just saw... something move. Over there in the distance."

Slogg turned to look in the direction being indicated. He also detected movement. He focused hard, trying to make sense of what he could discern.

There appeared to be a myriad of small, hooded figures trekking as a bipedal group, each of their heads stooped low. Their gowns were of the deepest sapphire blue and all their features or faces were hidden. The large group swayed thymically side to side as they advanced forwards. The movement was purposeful and somewhat threatening in its solid monotony. However, none seemed aware of the landing party.

"Did *they* issue the distress call?"

"Hard to say Captain, but they are the nearest to the original source," replied Taroooc.

"Multimodal field-glasses please."

"I thought you brought them."

"Please could you surprise me one day in a *positive* way. Okay... we need to get a look at what we are dealing with here, so it's time we formed an Advancement Party. I shall protect the rear. Zero, you lead."

"Thanks..." said Zero, "Correction... but no thanks."

Slogg assessed the remaining crew. He questioned his own sanity for bringing the Second Officer and two security bowling pins. He turned to his Medical Officer.

"Yelyah Soss, you are reinstated as Medical Officer and Advancement Party Leader. Taroooc will accompany you."

"As you wish."

And so, on this very cold planet a very cautious Advancement Party was formed. Taroooc advised he would rather be in a Drinking Party underneath a table in Refreshment Bay Two. He stepped cautiously at the front with Yelyah, eyes fixed on their hooded quarry. The two security robots hummed behind. The Second Officer hid neatly behind Zero and Slogg brought up the rear, his eyes scanning the hills.

"Keep low," he hissed. "We need to know if these guys want help or conflict."

"I can't…" announced Zero abruptly.

Yelyah turned to understand Zero's concern.

Taroooc was caught off-guard and thumped into Yelyah's left shoulder. The two security robots clunked into Taroooc's back. This pile-up tumbled all four of them to the ground. Zero's metal toecap caught this lumbering group and he also careered forwards to hit the icy surface.

"…keep low. I am… too tall," he finished.

"Then again," he corrected as he hit the ground, "it would appear I am not any more."

This commotion earned the attention of the distant hooded creatures, who stopped immediately in their tracks. Each raised their heads so slighly, but not enough to reveal their faces. The movement had the effect of transforming them into sinister hooded creatures. One of whom clearly possessed a sizeable gun.

Slogg ducked behind the bulk of Zero to join the Second Officer.

"*Well*?" he squealed. "Anyone?"

"They could be hostile," Taroooc informed him.

"Amazing powers of deduction,"

"I just saw a Zenpo Nasty Thing," Yelyah called back.

This situation was tight, sudden, ridiculous and

self-induced. They lay in the middle of a barren wilderness, the only real cover provided by a giant silver robot visible for fifty kilotecs. Slogg's mind raced.

Had these beings issued the distress call? Was it a trap? Or a misunderstanding?

By now the whole party crouched behind Zero. Any clear view was obscured by the colossal recumbent robot.

"Zero," commanded Slogg, "What's your verdict? I need an assessment of the situation, risk scenario and likely outcome?". He anticipated a 26th generation refinement in robotics would possess its own multi-modal vision and accompanying scenario analysis algorithms.

Zero's head raised slightly, and what passed for its eyes slowly scoured the distance.

"It is actually O.K…" announced Zero.

"Good news…" said Slogg.

The robot turned to look at him in surprise.

"Just what I was hoping," finished Slogg. "Thank you."

Slogg stood to wave a hand, offering the universal peace gesture to his new allies. A gun was fired and Slogg was shot through the head.

"…W - 349" completed Zero, finishing his analysis of the Zenpo Nasty Thing's serial number.

Slogg's body hit the ground.

CHAPTER 9

Slogg was alarmed - in part because he had been shot through the head, but primarily because it had not killed him. It brought to mind surviving a prior incident he attributed to good luck, an oversized skull, and very small brain cavity.

To support this theory and extend his life insurance, he recently invested in a course of synthetic nano-adrenalin injections. These now activated, coursing through his veins to ensure he felt no pain under attack. The blended artificial coagulants also preserved blood loss.

He would need to wear a long fringe again.

He slipped back behind Zero. He touched his head where the projectile had entered to feel a newly damp, mushy scar forming.

"Fat lot of use you are!" he cursed the robot.

"Ball stick..." said Zero, "Correction. Ballistic analysis informs that Zenpo Nasty Thing…"

"Yes?"

"...was their latest model *Occasional Kill Weapon - Three Four Nine.*"

"Ah," put in Taroooc, "those are the guns designed to reduce lawsuits amongst regular infantry by introducing an element of chance when discharged."

"That makes no sense. *Occasional Kill Weapon?*"

"If you can never be sure it was your firearm that produced the kill, you can never be sued under any circumstances."

Slogg stared expressionless at Taroooc.

"Okay. We came here to collect a Peacefulness and Primacy Offering."

"A *what?*" challenged Yelyah.

"I'll explain another time. We landed unarmed, in

retrospect a bad decision. They…" he pointed to the distance, "have at least one gun. And it can occasionally kill. I suggest that… we mediate."

"Captain, I just saw a pink elephant."

"Shut up Yelyah."

"As you wish."

"As I was saying, I believe we should follow a non-aggressive course. I am assuming there is some misunderstanding here. Why would they drag us down here with a distress call and then proceed to *shoot* all of us?"

"They only tried to shoot you sir," Taroooc pointed out.

"Can't be all bad then," added the Medical Officer.

"Yelyah," said Slogg.

"Yes?"

"You're fired."

"As you wish."

"As I was saying..."

"Don't you want to hear about the pink elephant?"

"No! Please stop talking."

"As you wish."

"Captain," said Taroooc, who had taken the risk of popping his head up above Zero's frame to assess the situation. "I really think you should see this."

A wall of small, faceless beings covered head to foot in sapphire-blue hooded robes were advancing rhythmically towards the landing party at a slow pace, heads bowed, and each carrying a small device in hand at which they intently stared. Their pace and concentration suggested deep meditation. The hoods covered their eyes and features. One creature remained behind, head down but holding the oversized firearm at his side. The rest continued in their pulsing march forward.

The only countersign to the meditative, synchronised stream was the flicker of slender fingers tapping rapidly over the devices they held.

"Are they holding weapons?" demanded Slogg.

"It would seem not Captain," said Taroooc. "Their only weapon bearer has stayed behind."

"What are they doing?"

The wall of deep blue hoods came steadily closer into clear sight. They halted in unison within ten paces of Slogg and his landing party. Still their heads remained stooped, intent on the devices in their hand.

"I think I know who they are," said Taroooc.

"You do?"

"Yes Captain, I've read about them on Galakipedia and seen rare images on holoTV. They are a unique tribe. The Digitari."

"Who? *Digitari*?"

"Yes Sir. And I think they are communicating."

"Communicating. How?"

"Twit…" observed Zero.

Slogg fixed Zero with a steely gaze.

"TwiText sir," said Taroooc, "Zero is nearly there. They are possibly trying to reach us on TwiText. Or maybe BokkFace."

"But… those recmedia channels are obsolete."

"Not everywhere sir."

There was a faint ping, and Slogg noticed his portable ship's communicator light was flashing. He pulled it from his belt and turned its screen towards him expecting to see Deluxia calling from the bridge.

Instead of his Communications Officer he saw a tiny, pixelated flag with a number *1* etched on it, together with the following:

⚑ Gwofie wishes to connect with you on TwiText. You have no mutual friends with Gwofie.

"What does this mean Taroooc, and who the hell is Gwofie?"

"It's a TwiText message sir. Gwofie is trying to poke you."

Slogg closed his eyes. His childhood annums were strewn with wearying grandparental stories of how they communicated via digital devices. Always how wonderful and sleek these devices were, and always in preference to in-person, facial or auditory interaction. *Tapping not talking* was the mantra they lived by. His body yearned to scream at the leaden sky.

As he screwed his eyes together and craned his neck upwards, one diminutive, hooded creature broke ranks and approached to prod his device into Slogg's groin.

Slogg opened his eyes.

As he did so, the two hundred cloaked figures manoeuvered to surround Slogg and his crew. Their faces remained obscured. A faint glow from each device lit their hands and the rim of their hoods.

A pink elephant emerged behind them.

Slogg concentrated on the prodding to his groin. It registered as a short creature in the same sapphire-blue hood as his companions. Intricately interwoven into his hood cloth was a small, subtle digital display with *...GWOFIE...* scrolling across its indigo screen. The creature's gown also offered *Commander* stitched onto the shoulder, together with an obscure emblem.

Slogg forced a grin and examined Gwofie's device as it continued to nudge his nether regions.

"That thing you have there," Slogg asked, "is it dangerous?"

The creature's fingers flashed across the device. Another ping emanated from Slogg's communicator. The message on his screen changed to:

Mine or yours?

This was followed with another prod.

"Yours!" coughed Slogg, "And do you mind not prodding me there."

He stepped backwards.

Another ping and another message.

My name is Commander Gwofie.

"That's a nice little name." commented Slogg.
Ping.

It's not a **little** name!

The creature moved forward with another prod and its fingers skitted across the device in a blur.
Ping.

It is short [autocorrection] an abbreviation for Gwofeelulplexipus The Large Nosed. That takes too long to type so it is shortened [autocorrection] curtailed to Gwofie. As an additional observation, I do not possess a large nose.

Ping.

But my uncle has.

Slogg stared down speechless at the little hood. There was still no sign of his face, nor that of any of his companions.
Ping.

U R tall aren't U.

"Yes," agreed Slogg with the statement, though unimpressed with the grammar.
Ping.

Scuzzball!

Slogg stared at his communicator screen for a few extra seconds to reread the statement.

"I beg your pardon!"

As Slogg spoke another pixelated icon appeared beneath this message depicting a hand with thumbs up. An accompanying message read:

👍 This post has 109 likes

Without looking from beneath his hood, the Gwofie creature raised his device away from Slogg's groin to point it between his eyes. A red glow radiated from its edge as Gwofie reached his fingers to blindly tap another message.

Ping.

What R U doing here Lofty?

"*Lofty*! Okay, this has gone far enough," declared Slogg, "We answered your distress call."

There was no ping.

There was a very long silence.

Slowly a few of the creatures tucked their devices into hidden pockets and stood in awkward stillness.

Gwofie then lowered the device from Slogg's viewpoint and towards his own lap. His fingers flashed across its screen.

Ping.

The hooded creatures a moment ago pocketing their devices frantically grappled through their cloaks to retrieve them. However, the message was for Slogg.

Whoops!

Sorry about that. LOL.

"Sorry!" Slogg barked, sensing the tables were turning. "What do you mean *sorry*? And who is Lol?"

I believe that is the universal form of apology.
👍 This message has 67 likes

It dawned on Slogg.
"So it *was* your distress call!"

Yes ☺

"And when we answer it you shoot me through the head?"

Oops. ☹

"That's the way you greet your rescuers?"

It was an **Occasional** Kill Weapon.
👍 This message has 12 likes and 1 dislike

"Which occasionally *kills*!"
Silence. Then…

☺

Slogg had the upper hand but he was tiring of the conversation.
"You do *not* seem to be in any distress. And will you please stop this TwiText charade and look at me."
Ping.

But we are in distress!

"So why attack the rescue party?"

Because you were tall ☺

"Tall!"

"Yes. Lofty. And... because you speak freely and comfortably to each other without the need for Bokkfacing TwiText.

"What?"

"You are lanky and lack inhibitions. Scuzzballs
👍 This message has 77 likes and is trending

Slogg's patience ran out.

"Right! Gwofie, if that's your name, you can't go around the universe killing everyone who happens to be able to see over your head. It's just not decent and it's not practical." said Slogg, inadvertently staring above a sea of faceless hooded creatures with heads bowed to their devices and fingers a blur of activity.

"And every single species of the Galactic Core I have met so far has no problem with face-to-face communication. So please... *look* at me."

There was a slight pause. Gwofie's fingers flew to his screen.

Ping. Ping. Ping ping ping ping...

But it's the universe's fault in the first place. Before the Digitari were introduced to the Galactic Core, we believed ourselves to be an effusive, statuesque race with athletic bodies, a decent analogue mobile infrastructure, and a love of literature, long walks and quiet contemplation. Then up pop a few Galactic Core representatives and we get *Sorry lads, you are ~~shorties~~ [autocorrection] vertically challenged*. Then they give us our Peacefulness and Primacy Offering to help us progress from 5G to 6 and 7, and provide instantaneous updates for Bokkface, TwiText and Toktikker. As a bonus they threw in some free Glossplastik phablets with our 5G plan. We try to ignore the insults, install 5G, and attempt to keep calm and carry on. But... to cut a long evolution short, once a single Digitari looks down to check for non-existent TwiTexts on their new phablet, we all start to fear we are missing out. We move very quickly from quiet reflection and enjoying the moment, to develop *The Fear of Empty Time*. We need to be engrossed... or pretend to be engrossed. Something must be happening somewhere that requires our attention to appear as important as our brethren. So, my dear Lofty, if I look up at you now - and there is the merest pause in our conversation – my companions will surmise I have no one to interact with but you. The *Fear* will kick in, and that... would amount to Bokkfacing suicide. Init. ☺

Slogg stared at the little man's hood unable to speak. The severe cold bit his neck again and he shivered.

"The *Fear of Empty Time*," he repeated. "I'm so sorry."

It threatens us constantly. But I'm the one who should apologise again. Anyway, most of us are in counselling. Albeit virtually, on our devices. The irony.

The digital display woven into his hood changed from *...GWOFIE...* to a sad face icon.

"I see," said Slogg. He inhaled deeply and turned to stare at Taroooc.

"Thoughts?"

"Er..."

"Not too difficult for you is it? Am I to suffer *The Fear of Empty Time* waiting for an answer?"

"Well... given our mission and your destiny, we could ask them what they are doing on this planet," suggested Taroooc.

Slogg turned back to Gwofie's faceless hood.

"You heard the man. Why are you here – in this godforsaken Braevitchkan solar system?"

The sad face icon disappeared from the hood.

Ping.

We were on an interstellar mission at the request of the Jockey Monks. We'd just updated the navigation app. Then our ship developed a fault as we came though their atmosphere. We had to force an early landing. We tried calling the monks but that was hopeless. We panicked and launched our distress call. And then, it turns out, we'd actually landed next to their monastic headquarters anyway.

"You were on a mission?" inquired Slogg. He waited for the reply.

Actually, yes. You may know, the Jockey Monks have an aversion to talking – it interferes with their drinking and horse racing. Well, same here! And so they identified the Digitari as the perfect species to assist. We have been asked to remove the majority of pink elephants that plague their planet.

"What?" Slogg managed.
A pause, and a flurry of digital dexterity.

Apparently, in their constant quest for brewing strength and perfection, a small sect evolved bizarre telegenerative powers.

"Telegenerative?"

Yes, the ability to create any type of matter from nothing. By simple, pure focused imagination, these monks can now produce the most flavoursome hops, finest yeast, precision fermenting tanks, you get the idea. And their beer just gets better... and stronger.

"Purists dedicated to their craft. Okay, I can almost accept this, but where do the *pink* elephants come in?"
Tappitappitiptaptiptaptaptaptippitap... ping ping ping

I was coming to that. It seems the evolved telegenerative powers are not exclusive to the conscious imagination. As well as being the finest, Braevitchkan beer is also the strongest in the universe, and the monks consume a *lot*. As they drift gently into their stupor, the telegeneration has also produced an excess of revolving rooms and, bizarrely, pink elephants.

"This is... ridiculous."

But true. The revolving rooms are being snapped up by the restaurant and hospitality industry, however it seems no one has any use for a pink elephant, and they have become a nuisance.

Slogg imagined his own telegenerative powers. At this instant he would have manifested a small hotel with a secure and beautiful master suite, immensely plush bed, deep pillows and a large holoTV filling one wall. Then he sighed a heavy sigh and asked:

"So, what's your payback for removing these elephants?"

Ping.

As much Braevitchkan beer as we can carry.

Slogg allowed himself a while to process this statement.

"Wait. So, you have a ship full of Braevitchkan beer? Nearby?"

Yes, or we're about to. We were loading the elephants and beer when you distracted us. But we still have a problem with the navigation app. We're tappers and shunters, but we're not software engineers.

A smile grew across Slogg's face. "Well, we are on a mission also. I have a destiny inducting a planet into the Galactic Club. And just guess what my Peaceful and Primacy Offering needs to be?

No idea.

"Let's walk and talk Commander Gwofie. I may be able to make you an offer you can't refuse. Where's your ship?"

Shall I TwiText you the location?

"No," exhaled Slogg, "just lead the way."

And so, the show had begun.

They reached the brow of a hilltop and descended its icy slopes towards a hulking spaceship and the makeshift Digitari camp. Slogg explained their need for Braevitchkan Beer and his counteroffer of software engineers to fix Gwofie's navigation app. The deal was struck as they entered the camp and strange sights began to greet the landing party.

Ping.

Welcome
This message has 42 likes

Several giant cages dotted the scene containing two or three pink elephants in each. More cages held crates of Braevitchkan beer.

As backdrop a midsized starship steamed from its vents. Its outer skin was a wonderous patchwork of hieroglyphs and small display screens streaming Twitext and Bokkface feeds.

To one corner of the camp stood another even more unexpected sight.

On its own gleamed a gilded hemi-spherical dome. It was perfectly smooth and featureless, except for a four-letter word pulsing rhythmically at its apex. The neon word said *GOSH*.

"What is that?" asked Slogg finally, pointing to the dome.

That's Gosh Bordomm. I can send you a link to his TwiText profile if you want.

"Who?"

As in *GOSH BORDOMM - Saviour of Northern Andromeda.* Here... *gww.galactipedia.uni/goshbord*

"I thought he was a superhero myth."

More Megastar. His words ☺

Gwofie led the party past this and on towards his stricken vessel. It dawned on Slogg he had not been in contact with his own starship since arriving. Pulling out his communicator he swiped away Gwofie's messages and reopened his secure WalkyTalky app.

"Slogg to ship. Slogg to ship. Are you receiving? Over."

Silence.

"I repeat, Slogg to ship. Are you receiving? Over."

A reply came through the ether.

"Hi. This is Deluxia. I'm sorry I'm not around at the moment. Please leave a message after the tone. Thank you. *Beep*."

Slogg raised his head to the sky, sighed, and then shivered.

It was still a very cold planet.

CHAPTER 10

Zero stood beside a plume of hot steam issuing from the Digitari's grounded starship. The white vapour swirled around his silver thighs, rose through his metallic groin up to his angular torso. It dulled the chrome sheen as it condensed on the cold Kolidium and finally played before his domed head as it disappeared into the thin air. Condensation formed on Zero's arms, and tiny water trickled down the metal in their own irregular patterns, to create crystal clear dew drops on the ends of his fingers. A greying, weak sun shone through the cold atmosphere causing the drops to glimmer faintly as they fell to the hard earth.

Taroooc observed this tranquil, picture-book scene as he walked by with Gwofie and Slogg. "What are you doing?" he asked.

"Rusting." said Zero.

"Oh. Why?"

"Beak...." said Zero, "oz... it's the only way.... I can weep corn *click whirr*... Correction, keep warm."

Taroooc carried on his way.

Once inside, after a short walk through the defective Digitari starship they reached its small bridge, which was very dark and a small panel of multi-coloured lights provided the only faint glow.

Taroooc followed Gwofie and Slogg as both appeared to stumble simultaneously and a rattling of beer bottles could be heard underfoot. Taroooc paused, unable to see in the dimness.

Ping.

Pull the piece of string above you with a knot tied in the end.

In the gloom Taroooc read his communicator's

screen and groped over his head. He found something chord-like. He pulled it.

Somewhere a toilet flushed.

Not the chain! The next one to it.

Taroooc fumbled and found another string to pull. A light came on.

"Ah, that's better," said Slogg.

They were standing beside a sweep of control panels embedded in a long, smooth, undulating desk. This slowly curved upwards with more switches, lights and small, touch-sensitive display screens.

This counter though, was not as sleek and junk free as its ergonomic designers intended. It was teeming with hundreds of pieces of string - each connected to a switch on the panel. As their eyes moved up to the ceiling, Slogg and Taroooc observed it too had the same strings dangling at irregular intervals.

It was cheap, coarse, brown string.

Ping.

Good eh?

"Good?" said Slogg. "Different."

"Unique." said Taroooc, seeing his recently pulled chord still swaying gently above his head. It was fixed with what appeared to be glue, to a slim light switch.

Gwofie jumped to pull a piece of string attached to the long desk console. Three display units flickered to life. One showed a diagram titled *Principal Navigation Units*. He then unclipped a long slender pole from beneath console and used it to touch the display. There was a flicker and an area magnified to show a flowchart and subroutines, some sections of which flashed red.

Ping.

Before he looked at his communicator, Slogg spoke.

"Gwofie. It's just the three of us in here, and none of your colleagues. Please, can we dispense with the screens and typing and just... *talk*."

The slender fingers went instinctively to his screen, but then froze. A silence hung in the air. *Empty time*.

Then the tiniest voice spoke from under the hood.

"But what if... I don't have anything to say? What will I *do*?"

"You don't need to have anything to say. Or anything to do. I might speak, Taroooc might, you might. Questions, answers, statements, observations, responses jokes, gaps. And possibly some *Empty time*. It's called a normal conversation."

Gwofie paused. Then he slowly lay down his device on the console before him. His fingers stayed with it a few more seconds and then... he let go.

Slogg and Taroooc discerned a small intake of breath. The slender fingers rose to his hood which he pulled back over his head to reveal a diminutive skull covered in translucent grey skin. Beneath the skin veins and capillaries were clearly visible distributing white blood around the cranium. Red eyes with vivid black pupils looked up at Slogg.

"Well... this is different," said Gwofie.

"Not for us," replied Slogg.

Gwofie looked up at the Captain with a surprisingly mournful expression.

"We are *trying* to evolve you know. We are aware of the situation we've got ourselves into."

"Good to hear."

"Case in point..." said the little voice, "we have upgraded our devices to include cameras."

"Okay... not exactly revolutionary, but a move forward perhaps," said Slogg, unsure where the conversation was going. Gwofie seemed keen to prove a point, and perhaps exercise his vocal chords for the first time in a very long while.

"You see, we spend so long looking downwards, a new idea is to use our device cameras to share pleasing photographs of any green meadow, turf or lawns we come across." His face beamed at the thought.

"Great," said Slogg flatly, nonplussed by the Digitari interest in green space.

"I know it's a small thing but its progress. We have a new app beyond TwiText, to share these pictures and type in little comments to go with them."

"Really?" Slogg wanted to move on.

"We call it InstaGrass."

Silence.

"I see, okay. Anyway Gwofie, moving onto this navigational issue…"

"Also! We plan to remain inclusive across our generations, so we have a beta test sharing family snaps, especially to encourage our elders and matriarchs. We hope to promote continued communication amongst the Digitari's senior citizens. There's a new app for that as well."

"Let me guess," offered Slogg.

"Please."

"InstaGran."

"Well done."

"Please Gwofie, can we move on?" Slogg pointed at the screen in front of them. "What's that you're showing us here?"

"Ha. Well, that's where the problem is with our navigation. You see it should be easy to fix," stated Gwofie, "but we've run out of these long, thin, brown bits."

"I beg your pardon?" said Slogg.

"Bloody discrimination if you ask me." said the little Digitari. "Ooh, profanity. It feels *so* much better saying it than typing it. *Bloody discrimination!* Wow. "

Slogg smiled sympathetically at him.

"Discrimination?" enquired Taroooc.

"Yes. Those *damn* G6 Starshipbuilders," continued Gwofie with his cursing. " Damn, damn, damn them! This is fun! *Daaaaamn!* They completely ignored the fact that we were shor... we were..."

"Vertically challenged?" offered Slogg.

"...and delivered a starship for the average height species." He was getting the hang of it now. "When we complained they smiled smugly and said *Plenty of leg room.* Sod them. At least, that was our verdict. So, we developed our own upgrades to cope. It's mainly my idea and I'm thinking of calling it *S-tring.* There you go. Phew! Not too technical I hope?"

"*String*?" repeated Slogg.

"S-tring, but yes. The Galactic patent has just been applied for so don't bother making any sketches. We should be hearing very soon."

"Er..." Slogg then decided it would be better for all concerned if he left some *empty time.* In fact, he envied the Digitari for leading such a sheltered existence.

Gwofie pulled down on the same piece of string in a movement intended to switch off the displays. However, the switch now needed flicking up, and this was impossible from his position.

"Of course," said Gwofie observing his guest's unease, "there's still a bit more development work to be done," and he leaned over to retrieve his long stick.

Slogg decided to help and reached across the diminutive Digitari to flip the switch off.

Gwofie scoffed loudly. He then pulled his hood back up to conceal his face. He grabbed his device from the console and went to leave.

Ping.

"Lanky git!"

Having been shown the basics of the ship's navigation systems, Slogg and Taroooc agreed their software engineers could feign a repair. Slogg negotiated eighty crates of Braevitchkan beer as compensation. He was very pleased. Business was settled, his appropriate Peacefulness and Primacy Offering was secured, and he had avoided any interaction with the Proltoid Jockey Monks. *Win-win* as his Classics lecturer Fid Fadood might have said.

The landing party began to make their way across the frozen landscape to a clearing, ready for removal from the planet by the Teleport Stream. Zero followed reluctantly from his make-shift sauna, creaking vaguely at the joints.

As they passed the gilded dome at the camp's perimeter the *GOSH* sign pulsed and a door hissed open. A man stood before them dressed top to toe in a gloss white, figure-hugging tunic with a high emerald collar. A similar coloured cape fluttered at his back. His height significantly exceeded that of Slogg and Taroooc and almost tipped Zero. His chest and shoulders were vast, though the green collar wrapped around a head far too small for the rest of the body. The letters *GB* were embossed in the middle of his gleaming torso.

"Hi," said Gosh.

"Hello," said Slogg, introducing himself, "Captain Slogg, this is Biophysics Officer Taroooc. Nice to meet you, but I'm sorry… we are leaving."

Gosh Bordomm's eyes lit up.

"Can I help?" asked Gosh.

"Sorry?"

"I'm Gosh Bordomm - Saviour of Northern Andromeda. I can fly."

He proved it by hovering a few feet above the ground.

"And save lives… fight crime?"

"It's alright," said Slogg, "we're good."

"But I am a *superhero*," put in Gosh. He subconsciously licked his index finger and smoothed over both of his eyebrows.

"Really?" started Taroooc.

"We don't need any help!" interrupted Slogg. "Thank you."

He tipped his chin up, indicating his landing party onward to the icy foothills, back to their starting point. They started to resume their walk.

"One minute..." said Gosh.

Slogg glanced at the Saviour of Northern Andromeda, who now carefully positioned himself high on a nearby rock, slightly angled to their view. Slogg noted Gosh was very deliberately sucking in his stomach.

"I am sure I can help?"

"As I've said already, we don't need any."

"Are you absolutely sure?" pressed Gosh, extending his chin to emphasize his jawline. "As a superhero I have laser eyes to cut any metal, and retractable talons to... dice vegetables?"

"I'm sorry Gosh, we are not in need."

"I can spin a web... any size."

"Look..." exclaimed Slogg.

"Okay," cut in Gosh. He stepped down from the rock. Slogg followed his landing party as they walked on. Gosh hurried to Slogg's side, his demeanour softening and his voice quietened. He struggled with his next words. He bent low to Slogg's ear.

"...it's just that... could you help *me*?"

"Sorry?"

"Could I hitch a lift?" pleaded Gosh.

"A lift?"

"Yes, away from this planet. It's bloody freezing you know."

"I thought you were a superhero. I thought you could fly."

"Not intergalactically. You see, I've messed up a

bit," confessed Gosh.

"A bit?"

Gosh looked at Slogg and widened his eyes but remained silent.

"If you want our help, I need more," said Slogg.

"Okay, okay," Gosh whispered, "I'm sort of... on the run."

"*On the run*! From whom?"

"Sshhh! From the Andromedan Revenue Service... and the Galactic Bureau of Investigation."

"Tax?"

"Well... more like tax efficiency."

"Tax evasion. Ha! The ARS and GBI... that's some heavy stuff Gosh."

"It's completely unwarranted and unnecessary. Have you heard of a ULSZ?"

"A what?"

"Exactly! Neither had I. It's an Ultra-Low Superhero Zone..."

"Ultra Low..."

"Superhero Zone. Apparently, some planets this side of the Galaxy are so congested with superheroes, the Galactic Core implemented a daily charge. We have to pay one hundred and ninety Geltoes a day, just to exist. I was on Neerizitt Six, quietly doing my shtick and saving lives. No one told me! I didn't find out for two annums, and by then it was too late!"

"So what happened?"

"The ARS came calling... and fined me. I was already struggling to pay the Higher Powers Tax, just because of the laser eyes and the fact I can fly. So here I am."

"Why here?"

"I panicked and ran. The Digitari were passing and I bought a ticket out. They gave me a discount saying I could help flick some switches. But now I'm sick of their heightist jokes. And their air of resentment is palpable."

They had reached the brow of the hilltop and approached the spot where the Teleport Stream would extract the landing party from the planet.

Slogg sighed

"I'm sorry Gosh, but…"

"I'm planning to pay the tax and the fine. I just need a bit more *time*. The ARS have now brought in the GBI, and I'm wanted. For something I knew nothing about. Captain, *please*. If I can just hitch a lift."

"We're on a mission Gosh, and a tight schedule."

"Drop me anywhere along the way. I'll work in your kitchens, dicing meat and veg."

He held up his hand a flicked up his long fingers. Sharp talons flashed instantly from the knuckles.

They had formed a circle ready for the Teleport Stream. Zero creaked into the rear, Yelyah, Taroooc, the Second Officer and the two bowling pins bunched together in front.

Gosh retracted his talons.

"Look…" said Slogg, exasperated.

"Okay… do you have any HR issues?" interrupted Gosh.

"*What*?"

"I'm retraining as a humanoid resources consultant. There's lots of money in it to repay my fines. I just need enough dark energy bandwidth to download next season's course."

"We're multi-species Gosh, not just humanoid. And we have to go."

"Okay, okay, final offer. This cape…"

Gosh reached round to hold up a section of the finest, shimmering emerald fabric that flowed down his back.

"… it's pure Ireenium."

There was an intake of breath from Taroooc and Yelyah.

"You can have it," said Gosh.

"The whole cape?" challenged Slogg.

Gosh exhaled slowly and deeply.

"Yes."

"Ok, jump in."

"Really?" squealed Gosh. He then hovered a little above the ground.

"It's okay Gosh, you don't need to impress us anymore."

"I'm sorry Captain, it happens sometimes when I get excited."

Slogg wanted to hear no more. He opened his communicator and spoke to the Beam Controller, asking that they be removed from the planet with one additional, extra-large passenger.

Gosh huddled in next to Zero.

Slogg sighed his millionth sigh.

As he was sucked up into the sky by a swirling cloud of electrons, he could think of only one word. Ireenium[14].

---

[14] Ireenium is the rarest metal in the current known Universe, mostly traded as minute swatches of lustrous green cloth just a few molecules thick. Marketed as a luxury for aeons under the slogan *Ireen, Y'Know What Ah Mean*, it is so devastatingly difficult to mine that, ironically, the energy and resource expenditure required to prospect and recover it, far exceed the actual value of the metal dug out. Whole planets have donated their mantles, ecosystems and existences to its excavation. As a result, a digital currency derivative *Ireencoin* came into being, based on the constant growth multiples witnessed in the metal's exorbitant price. Ireencoin's value then surpassed even its base metal's worth because the currency was so fantastically rare, it did not even exist.

CHAPTER 11

Back on board, warm sickly drinks greeted the party as they arrived. Zero now filled the empty time in his conversation with squeaks from his joints. He was escorted back to Dzkk's loading bay by one of the maintenance crew. The omnipotent old man remained onboard as his Eggkraft stayed resolutely un-fixable. Yelyah willingly returned to her sickbay sanctuary.

Gosh Bordomm accompanied Slogg and Taroooc to the bridge. As well as securing the Ireenium cape, Slogg was intrigued to see if the superhero's HR training could uncover any insight amongst his immediate reports.

The two security robots hummed away for a herbal bath and recharge.

As they entered the bridge Deluxia quickly zipped her make-up case.

"Busy?" asked Slogg, resuming his Captain's seat. He beckoned Taroooc and Gosh to join him.

Gosh smiled at Deluxia and hovered a little.

"Taroooc," said Slogg, "select a software engineer and app developer to go down to Gwofie's ship to fix their navigation. Choose the best, so it's damn quick."

Deluxia was in love and her tail swished gently side to side. Her prevailing strange taste in the opposite species was making this newly arrived gloss white hulk very attractive. Even his small head matched her exotic preferences.

Slogg turned to Gosh.

"You offered to help with HR. Let's start with a performance management assessment here on the bridge. You've got 30 minutes before my engineers return and then we leave. This is Deluxia…"

Deluxia had not really listened to Slogg, having become severely distracted. Hearing her name, she noticed a faint sparkle in the superhero's eye as his boots reconnected with the floor. She sensed some subtle conversation was necessary.

"Gosh…" she exclaimed admiringly, "you are *very* tall. I'm Deluxia Moe Delle."

"I'm flattered you recognized me," smiled Gosh Bordomm. "Pleased to meet you," and again he hovered again at a slight angle, holding in his stomach.

Bemused by his response, Deluxia pressed on.

"Are you going to introduce yourself?"

"Bordomm." he nodded.

"No honestly, I am genuinely interested."

"I'm Gosh Bordomm."

"Ah, now I get it," said Deluxia. "And are you from Braevitchka?"

"It was just a short visit," answered Gosh, smoothing another eyebrow.

"Ok. And before that?"

"My home planet, Neerizitt."

"Near where?"

"No, Neerizitt."

"I see. So, it's near Izitt," checked Deluxia. "I've not been to Izitt."

"No, it's Neer… yes… that's right, Neerizitt."

"You are a long way from home then," observed Deluxia.

"Well yes, roaming with those Digitari, and their little ship, took fifty-six lightdays of non-stop travel. And not one of them would even *look* at me, never mind talk."

"Gosh…" commiserated Deluxia, "Boredom!".

"Yes dear, what is it?"

"You just told me. It's a planet near your planet."

"What is?"

"Izitt. I really don't know it that well."

Gosh stopped hovering and reconnected with the floor. Slogg also tuned into their conversation. He rotated his immense chair and interrupted.

"Deluxia, I've heard all I need to. The time is up on your performance review."

"Really. Is it?"

"No, Neerizitt," said Gosh.

"What is?" demanded Slogg.

"No, sorry. I've never heard of that one," said Gosh.

Deluxia suddenly understood. She raised her eyes to the ceiling, having quickly tired of the superhero.

"Oh gosh…" she sighed, "Boredom!"

"Yes dear? What do you want?"

Another deep exhale from Deluxia followed.

"Oh gosh, Gosh. You started out so promising."

The huge screen dominating the bridge displayed an impressive view as a frail sun christened a new day within the Braevitchkan system.

The HR performance review had moved on to the First Officer and Gosh sat absent mindedly picking imaginary lint from his gloss tunic, whilst feigning conversation.

"Any news from the engineers yet?" Slogg asked Taroooc.

"We only sent them down a short while ago Captain."

"I know that, but the quicker we can get out of here the better," said Slogg, "and… I've got a destiny."

His predestination swam back into view. The masters of the universe had ordained him as baton carrier for a planet bearing intelligent life.

Pride welled back into his chest.

"Ask them again Taroooc."

Meanwhile the First Officer squealed and kicked his chair backwards. The commotion caught Slogg's attention.

"I can't do this! Yes... I am happy and yes, I am productive. And yes, I feel fear. But I feel it *all the time*. It's not got anything to do with the job!"

"I understand, I understand," said Gosh Bordomm. "It's important I understand the basis of your fear. Imagine you're in a desert, walking along the sand, when all of a sudden you look down and see a tortoise..."

"Do you make these questions up, Mr Bordomm? Or do they write them down for you?" pleaded the First Officer.

"You're not helping," said Gosh.

"That's enough!" intervened Slogg. "Thank you Gosh. It's okay Bleep, the interview is over."

The First Officer stormed away to a distant corner to hold the back of a chair tightly. He hid his face from the rest of the bridge.

"The engineers are back onboard Captain," reported Taroooc. "Fixing the Digitari's app was quick job apparently,"

"Ok, some good news at last," said Slogg. "Did they say what was wrong with their ship?"

"A piece of string had broken?"

"Ha!"

"Ok Walta, get us out of here. Maximum superluminal drive. Sector Alpha C, seven zero nine. Hypercube sixteen.

"Aye, Sir," beamed Walta, dexterously rotating his favourite notched dial. "Here we gooooo..."

The ship began accelerating smoothly and rapidly into a long arc.

"And," continued Taroooc, the large gap between his eyes seeming to widen further, "the engineers have news they brought back a present from the Digitari."

"What kind of present?"

"Well…" paused Taroooc, "Perhaps it's a joke."

"What kind of present?" Slogg persisted. He felt his temporary euphoria beginning to wane.

"A pink elephant."

Slogg's threadlike smile disappeared completely.

A few moments later the huge starship heaved itself out of the Braevitchkan solar system and into superluminal ether. The powerful Krystaltachyon engines roared as they overcame quantum relativity. Behind them, lurking in a vast void holding the first four planets, a mid-sized starship made its final preparations to leave beer, monks, racetracks, and a bitter landscape. Its complement of pink elephants (minus one) would provide currency - it was hoped - somewhere in the universe.

Slogg, enlightened but not amused by the recent events, pondered on what they were going to do with their own pink elephant the engineers miraculously smuggled aboard. It was now stuck in a corridor close to the Teleport bay.

With the final act of his destiny playing out, Slogg decided it time to visit Dzkk once more and report progress. As he stood to leave the bridge a thought struck him.

"Gosh," he called.

"Yes, can I help?" asked Gosh employing the eyebrow lick, "I can fly."

"How would you, as Saviour of *Whatever*, like to meet one of the universe's Masters?"

"Not Mabel?"

"No, not Mabel. Follow me."

"Never heard of him," said Gosh.

"Who?" quizzed Slogg.

"Folomee. Is he a recluse God?"
"Just get in the lift please."
Schtip.

They reached the loading bay and the huge silver doors did not open. Again. A sequence of light jumps on its pressure mat also proved futile.

Slogg smiled at Gosh.

"It's okay. I've had problems with this one before. A sucker for punishment aren't you?"

"No," said the door.

"Open up!"

"No," said the door.

"I'm ordering you."

"No."

"Are you listening?"

"No."

"I see. It's stuck in a *No Loop*. Probably deliberate," Slogg explained, "It's a subroutine feature normally available to the main controller for extreme emergencies. You're in a *No Loop* aren't you?"

"No," said the door.

"Can you say anything else?"

"No."

"Okay, so if I order you to open now, you'll stay shut?"

"No... *oooohh*"

Schtip.

"...Crap!"

The door opened.

"Sometimes," mused Slogg, "human logic beats the drivel out of computer logic."

They walked in.

The Eggkraft hung in the gantry. Zero was ever

present beside it. Light tapping and deep sporadic thudding could be heard from the vessel's interior. The neck of the giant robot squeaked as he turned to look at Slogg and Gosh.

"Nice to see you again Zero," said Slogg.

"Rot...ating my joints is a little diff...icult," croaked the robot.

"Oh dear," said Slogg, as he sidled past the silver beast. Gosh followed him stopping briefly to check his reflection on Zero's chrome torso.

Inside the Eggkraft the all-powerful Dzkk lay beneath a grey console with a photon wrench in his stubby left hand, radiance screwdriver between his teeth, and his right hand deep inside the guts of wiring.

"Hello!" called Slogg tentatively into the dim interior.

"Ah, Captain Slogg. Do come in. What have done to my robot?"

"Sorry?" queried Slogg.

"Why, the squeaks, moans and groans he now issues forth are most annoying," Dzkk explained.

"So… are yours, chicken man!" came a distant metallic voice.

"Insolence!" hissed Dzkk, "No respect these days. I remember when I was young... no, that won't really work anymore will it."

He looked past Slogg and watched a large, muscled frame squeeze through the small hatchway.

"Who is this with you?"

"This is Gosh Bordomm," announced Slogg.

"Who?"

"Gosh Bordomm - Saviour of… *the Whatever*."

"Northern Andromeda," corrected Gosh, "Can I help? I can fly."

"Can you fix Eggkrafts?" Dzkk asked him flatly.

"Well…"

"Then go and save the Northern Andromeda. I've

heard that it probably needs saving."

"But…"

Dzkk ignored him and continued towards Slogg.

"Remind me Captain, once this assignment is all over, to increase my omnipotent powers to include routine interstellar shuttle maintenance."

"Assignment?" inquired Gosh.

"That is what I said."

"And?"

"The Captain here has a destiny, to bring another planet into the Galactic Core. The first for a while."

"And which planet might that be?" asked Gosh.

Dzkk told him.

"That one!" exclaimed Gosh, "Oh dear. Oh no."

"What's wrong?" asked Dzkk, "It's harmless. Mostly®."

"But it is back towards… *home*."

"Home?"

"It's close to my home planet. I can't go back, yet."

"Where is that?" asked Dzkk.

"Neerizitt."

"Near where?"

"No, Neerizitt."

Slogg interrupted. "Please gentlemen, not again. Let us… move on."

Gosh briefly explained.

"For a variety of technical reasons relating to the ARS and GBI I cannot risk travel within any sectors close to my home planet."

"Well, I'm sorry," began Dzkk, "but it is the Captain of this starship's destiny, and as such it has to be fulfilled. And that means, now."

"Then I'll have to leave," said Gosh, realizing as he spoke the words what the ramifications were.

"We need all the shuttles we've got," said Slogg. "You can't just leave, there's nothing to leave in."

A moment of silence ensued. Dzkk was preoccupied with one of Gosh's previous statements.

"Did you say ARS and GBI?" he asked. "Are you on the run?"

"On paper, yes," said Gosh.

"Captain!" began Dzkk. "This is dangerous. It could severely – *severely* – affect your mission and your destiny."

"He asked for help," said Slogg. "He also offered his cape."

"His cape?"

"Yes."

Dzkk eyed the garment in unexpected awe.

"Is it *Ireenium*?" he hissed.

"It very much is," beamed Gosh, "…all of it."

"Where are we?"

"What do you mean?"

"Where are we, our coordinates?"

"Well, we entered superluminal ether approximately…"

"We are just inside the Southern Andromedan Hemisphere," interrupted Gosh.

"How the hell did that happen!"

Dzkk turned immediately to Slogg.

"*Cops!*" hissed Dzkk.

Slogg was mystified and stunned into silence.

"Agreed," realised Gosh, "I should leave now."

"Captain, I suggest that Mr Bordomm is released from this ship instantly. We must *not* risk the destiny."

Slogg stared wide-eyed at both of them.

"Okay, I am Captain of this ship, and I admit that do not want to understand. But as Captain of this ship, I do know… that we possess not one spare shuttle craft to let Gosh simply fly away and never return."

"Take the Eggkraft," said Dzkk immediately.

"The Eggkraft!" exclaimed Gosh, "Really?"

"Give us the Ireenium cape and take my

Eggkraft."

"Are you sure?"

"If you can fix it, you can have it."

"Fix it! Gimme those tools. Before I got my superpower licenses, I used to spend annums as a child fixing anything and everything. Lightmonths and months in a shed, just me, nuts, bolts, wires, plugs, screws, circuits, a photon wrench and a radiance screwdriver…"

"Gosh," sympathised Dzkk, "boredom…"

"Yes," asked the superhero, "what do you want?"

"STOP!" shouted Slogg, "I've had enough."

"The Eggkraft?" checked Gosh.

"Yes. Take it."

"Right. You're on!" and he grabbed the wrench and screwdriver from Dzkk's thick fingers, ready to dive under the console.

"First the cape, please…" said Dzkk.

"Oh yes, of course."

"And would you like to take Zero as well?"

Gosh smiled a very broad, very thin smile and shook his head almost imperceptibly.

"Thank thuck for fat…" said Zero, "Correction…"

"It doesn't need correcting!" interrupted Dzkk. "Mr. Bordomm you will need the instruction manual and some of these tools…"

"Well, we'll leave you to it then Gosh," said Slogg. "I'm heading back to the bridge. Dzkk, can I buy you a drink? We're in superluminal drive and finally on our way. We deserve a toast. Destiny awaits!"

In the same superluminal ether, sixty lightminutes behind, blue and red lights began to flash in pursuit of Slogg's starship.

PART TWO

US

For time and the world do not stand still.
Change is the law of life.
1963, John. F. Kennedy

CHAPTER 12

1983

1st September
09:15am BST, London UK

The McDonald's juggernaut was long gone from north London.

An acrid smell of scorched bread strayed from the kitchen to open-plan living room. The sleeping body had woken slowly, stretched hard, scooped cold water from the tap onto its face, and was now recognisable as Nelson Staff. The burnt aroma could be traced to two black triangles of charcoal smeared with partially melted butter, one of which Nelson held in his hand as he sat at the makeshift breakfast bar. He would define these as toast if anyone asked him, but no one would because Nelson currently lived alone – temporarily. Why he was in this situation is a long story, and not this one.

A Heaven 17 T-shirt and cotton boxer shorts protected Nelson's modesty. His light brown close-cropped hair resisted any grooming and a suggestion of redness around his green-grey eyes was the only telltale of a night before.

He considered scrambled eggs, a streaky bacon sandwich, or butter-fried mushrooms. His stomach considered the Guinness, pizza, Cabernet Sauvignon, Caramac, sponge cake, cheese, grapes and milk he had devoured until the early hours watching overdue VHS video rentals. The fridge door remained closed.

Nelson shuffled to his bedside table and retrieved the envelope from beneath his Sony Walkman cassette player and a coffee-stained *Greetings from Cyprus* postcard.

The envelope contained a yellowing, typed memo clearly marked as *Private and Confidential*.

Nelson's 9 to 5 involved authoring technology articles for Sunday supplements. As an untrained journalist he was fortunate to land the role based on an unusual passion for the Sinclair ZX81 and an eloquent, vehement letter he penned to *Computing* magazine extolling its superiority over the new Commodore 64.

His current assignment played to these strengths, asking him to document the accelerating microcomputer industry, and his editor had deadlined a completed article submission by the coming weekend.

A day earlier, his research into the history of computers had led him deep in the nether regions of the local Swiss Cottage library. After checking the reference cards and following a quiet chat with the librarian, Nelson had approached a thick encyclopaedic tome and delicately separated this out. As its fusty cover had stuck to its siblings he experienced a sense of the archeological. He prised open the giant reference book, resisting the urge to blow imaginary dust from its pages. As he did so the envelope had fallen out.

The postmark was faint but readable as *1927*, and was imprinted across a row of ornate US postage stamps depicting the Liberty Bell 150th Anniversary. And… the letter was still sealed, as if it were waiting all the intervening fifty-six years for the right person to discover it.

Maybe it was a test. Or a prank? Nelson mused the possibilities as he looked carefully around to check if any eyes or cameras peered at him through the bookcases. He held the envelope delicately in his hand, contemplating whether he would be judged the *right person*.

Nelson dived in and read its contents. What he found made his eyes pop. He became so overwhelmed he technically committed theft, slipping the typed letter into his jacket pocket and bringing it home.

He now returned to the kitchen, finished his Tropicana orange juice and reached for the Kellogg's Frosties.

Inside the envelope was a formally typed memo and embossed heading displaying a *NASA* logo. The National Aeronautics and Space Administration of the United States of America was writing to a local scientist with the enchanting name of Doctor Oswald Grimaldi, based in Compayne Gardens, West Hampstead, London NW6. This wonderful coincidence excited Nelson since he lived just a few roads away. NASA thanked the doctor profusely for his recent comments on the newly revised rocket propulsion devices, and the calculations associating these to the projected Moon landings.

Nelson mused as the kitchen radio played UB40's *Red, Red Wine*. He preferred *The Earth Dies Screaming*. An over-excited competition winner asked the DJ to play *Life On Mars* by David Bowie, and Nelson scraped the last few sugary flakes from his bowl.

NASA had been very interested in reconnecting with Doctor Grimaldi at his earliest convenience, strangely referring to him multiple times as *Dog'2G*. To stress the private nature of the memo, its sender had included an intriguing *Top-Secret* stamp.

However, the most extraordinary feature was clearly typed twice on the letter heading, and again beneath the scrawled signature of a Mr J. Schuger, *Shu'6J*, Chief Scientific Officer, NASA Headquarters.

The DJ followed on with Bowie's *Changes* as Nelson cleaned out his bowl with a rinse under the cold tap.

He stared at the letter again.

The date that appeared twice:

20th September 1927.

1927!

Forty-two years before the first man stepped on the Moon.

"It's a fake," said Nelson to the oven, "or a bad typist."

No response, unsurprisingly.

"Okay, it simply has to be a fake."

He grabbed a corner of the letter and fanned it loosely backwards and forwards as he stared out his kitchen's large window frame. The peaceful road beyond was littered with parked Peugeots, Ford Orions and Austin Maestros, mostly commuters taking benefit of the free spaces and nearby tube station.

He could ignore it: name, date, address and collectible stamps. Drop it in the bin and move on. These ideas felt instinctively misguided and ran against all his impulses. The address on it was local and this presented an alternative approach: return it to its original owner. If he still existed.

Where would that get him? Nelson visualised the prospect of meeting an old Dr. Grimaldi and offering him his letter back.

"So..." said Nelson. This annoying ritual of talking to himself just after waking proved disturbing for anyone who happened to be around him at that time. It was a subconscious habit borne of living with a speechless gas appliance.

If there was the remotest chance of meeting anyone involved in the Moon landings, Nelson would jump at the prospect.

The trio of Bowie hits ended with *Starman*.

The shine was already dimming on Nelson's short journalistic career and his current deadlines were slipping.

A walk would clear his head. And if he were unsuccessful, he could always treat himself to lunch at the new McDonalds in Swiss Cottage[15].

"...let's *go!*"

On this premise Nelson left the flat immediately and impulsively. Twelve seconds later he was lucky to walk back through the gently closing door to wash, shave and put on the rest of his clothes.

---

[15] In the midst's of time, London gentry installed a toll gate, complete with keeper's cottage, on the main road leading from the City to the expanding village of Finchley. In 1806, as beer consumption began to generate far greater income than passing stagecoach tariffs, the gate was demolished and replaced by a tavern, constructed to mimic Swiss chalets of the era. The imbibing cognoscente flocked in, and the area became known by the portmanteau *Swiss Cottage*, partly from Londoner's imaginative apathy, and partly from their fondness towards misleading foreign visitors.

CHAPTER 13

West Hampstead is a district of London that was well served by Luftwaffe efficiency during the early 1940s. The era led to numerous bombsites, reconstruction, and pockets of incongruous, often brutal 1950s to 60s apartment blocks and public buildings, surrounded by row upon row of the original Edwardian four-storey houses. Then each of these impressive single homes now long since converted to multiple residential flats.

Grimaldi's address printed on the letter was a short walk for Nelson, and dressed in Adidas monochrome trainers, slim jeans and a light Harrington jacket, he soon found himself standing outside one of these blocks. A small outdoor lift beckoned, and he stepped in, pressing the button for the second floor. He checked his appearance in the scratched chrome mirror fixed to the lift wall and smiled at the scrawled graffiti message: *Stare at the numbers, shuffle your feet* **>>>** *and DON'T TALK!*

The lift gears ground into motion and it ascended painfully upwards. The doors opened unexpectedly one floor short. He stared at the small red button displaying 2. It remained lit and he pressed it again. Twice. He gave up the argument, walked out and took the stairs up another flight.

He walked out to a balcony with a left side railed over a concrete courtyard. On the right were six blue doors. The first door had an elderly man buckled over a dozen or so small plant pots clustered around the *Welcome* mat. He levelled his watering can and straightened to observe Nelson cautiously as he walked past him. Nelson instinctively smiled, but the old man remained stony faced. He continued to his target door towards the end of the balcony and knocked firmly.

From the inside there came the sound of bare feet on carpet and the door opened, but still on the chain. A young woman with deep brown eyes and wonderful dark brows peered out. Her brunette hair was soaking wet and wrapped an olive-skinned face with a fringe, then framed her cheekbones to just reach the nape of her neck. Water droplets fell onto her shoulders and Nelson could see she was dressed only in a bath towel.

"*Yes!*" she snapped, with the callousness of any human dragged from the midst of a hot shower to answer the door for a complete stranger. In particular one who was banging and ringing at the same time.

"Hello," said Nelson, "Doctor Grimaldi?"

"*Who?*"

"Doctor Oswald Grimaldi. I have a letter for you." He attempted to prove he was not a random voyeur by holding up the NASA letterhead. But the woman was clearly uninterested.

"There is no one of that name living here – and I've never heard of them," she declared.

Nelson looked at the door number and back at the letter. He glanced along the balcony to the lift and then back at the bath towel.

"But it is this address," he said, and then without really knowing why added, "Can I just come in?"

"*Certainly not!*" she said and slammed the door as hard as possible.

Nelson faintly heard the girl stomp away - presumably returning to the bathroom.

"It's not what you think," he called out.

He heard footsteps behind him. He turned to see plant-pot man approaching, eyeing him gravely.

"Have you been bothering young Miss Reagan?"

"No, no. Of course not. I seem to have the wrong place. No, I seem to have the right place but the wrong person. Not that there is anything wrong with her, no. She's lovely. She's just... *wrong*."

"Then who were you looking for?"

"Doctor Grimaldi."

"Doctor..."

"Doctor Grimaldi. I've got a letter. You see it has this address on it but... Oh, it doesn't matter," said Nelson and began walking miserably back to the lift.

The old man watched him a few moments waiting for the lift. He then said:

"It doesn't come to the second floor. Hasn't done for years, which keeps us all fit, so we don't complain. Anyway... he's dead."

"...*Sorry*?" said Nelson again.

"Doctor Grimaldi, he's gone. Dead presumably."

"You knew him!"

The old man walked towards his blue front door.

"Yes, I remember the old git... Eastern European I think, and strangely secretive. And you're right, he did live where Miss Reagan lives now... with his wife."

"He was married?"

"Yes, as far as I knew. But she left him, so we all heard. And that seemed to hit him very hard."

"I have a letter of his," offered Nelson, "but I don't suppose he'll want to be reading it now."

"Probably not," replied the old man, "I should think his eyesight's failed him completely after ten or more years underground."

"You mean he works on the Tube?" asked Nelson.

"No," said the old man. "I mean he's dead! Buried."

"I see, of course," apologized Nelson. "But... ten years ago?"

"At least. I used to do odd jobs around the house. He'd say *a shilling if you're willing*. Perhaps you should try that, you know..." the old man chuckled deeply and pointed back down the balcony. He made himself cough.

Nelson interrupted.

"So you say he was secretive. Did he ever give

102

you any clue about what he was hiding – or did you ever see anything?"

"Well..." said the old man, very pleased that someone was taking an interest in his stories, "I got *very* close once. You see, he used to ask me in to do things for him, plumbing mainly. Apparently, he had no idea about taps, cisterns and leaks. But, he would always clear down before I came in, you could tell. Boxes with locks on them, large pieces of paper rolled up tightly and tied, pens and drawing tools all neatly stacked. Big cigar butts in the ashtray. He loved his cigars. And then, he did his back in."

There was a pause as if the connection were obvious, but it wasn't.

"And so?" said Nelson finally.

"He asked me to pick up his post for a few weeks, from our letter boxes downstairs. Sometimes his back was so bad he'd give me a key to let myself in, but only after knocking first. This day I knocked, twice, then let myself in... and he's fast asleep on the couch in the living room with a half empty bottle of whisky. He always said it was to help the pain."

He took a step closer to Nelson and lowered his voice.

"I put his post gently down and as I crept out, I went past his study... and the temptation was too huge. It was such a strange room, full of old newspapers and empty bottles of all shapes. A long wooden trestle table filled one end, covered in rolled up papers. But..."

"Go on, said Nelson, taking his cue.

"But... one of these scrolls was fully opened and pinned down by a Marmite jar and a bottle of Glenfiddich. It's funny what sticks in the mind."

"It is," said Nelson.

"So, I spent a few minutes staring at this... well this, diagram. The only way I can describe it now is looking like the bottom end of some rocket booster – you know the up-ended funnel bit. And then suddenly, I knew he was standing behind me."

"Ouch. What happened?"

"I stood my ground and asked if I'd finally found what he'd been working on."

"Did he answer?"

"I remember it clear as day, he stared at me challengingly and said, in his Eastern European accent: *No, no, my friend, eeet's thee oldest treek in thee boook. I leave old diagram's een case someone snoop around thee flat.* Then he stubbed out his freshly lit cigar and told me to get out."

"And that was it?" asked Nelson.

"I'm afraid so. Mostly."

"Mostly?"

"Well... even though it was the early 60's there was a weird title on that giant sheet. I can still remember it."

Nelson's stare came up from the NASA letter he was holding. He looked direct into the man's eyes.

"What was written on it?" he demanded.

"The title said, *International Space Station.*"

"What the hell is one of those?" exclaimed Nelson.

The old man shrugged. Without his plant pots as immediate support, he expressed embarrassment at such a revelation, feigned distraction, shook his head and turned towards them.

"Anyway, that was a long time ago. Now it's going to be a hot day and my begonias are thirsty."

He went to his flowers, leaving Nelson to his thoughts.

CHAPTER 14

Underneath the Peak District, Cha'3E finished his presentation and replaced the laser pointer. The AI in the room lighting detected this combination and gently faded up the brightness whilst rolling the screen microfabric back into its ceiling recess.

He stood under the intricately carved owl on the wooden panel wall and smiled silently at his colleagues convened around the conference table. Zen lay in the corner.

It had gone well, and he started to detect slight but appreciative nods ripple round the room.

Dex'2O was first to speak.

"Love it. Starbucks, what a choice. What a name! And it's very different, which is great for our Directorate."

"Thank you Dex, I'm glad you liked it. As indicated, it's ready to go and needs just two Progressionaries on the *surface* to begin with, so minimal intervention. It will put us in a great position for *The Quit.*"

"That's the best bit. And our man… *Bill*… did I say it right…"

"Yes."

"…Bill is in Seattle already, so will he be briefed?"

"Of course."

"Great. Well, it gets my approval. Given the radical nature of this, can I ask what your second global intervention is going to be?"

"Sorry, do you mind waiting until the weekend Dex, as we'd planned. Emm and I are finalizing that particular coup's numbers."

"As you wish."

"Thanks. But I can assure you, it is also going to be very big."

CHAPTER 15

Nelson ignored lifts and graffiti and took the stairs. Even the jarring of a slow climb downwards did nothing to clear his mind. He chewed a bottom lip and stared at his striding feet as they thudded into the pavement. He crossed the road without thinking and a rare London cyclist almost struck him.

"Same to you," said Nelson, without looking up.

If he accepted they were working on moon-landing propellants in the late 1920s, why had it taken over forty years to become a reality? And what the on *Earth* is, or was, an *International Space Station*?

Nelson was perplexed about Grimaldi and his handiwork. But what puzzled him the most was, fakes or not, why hide away in West Hampstead and the lesser known 1960's monolith of Swiss Cottage library?

Questions. That was all he had.

He strolled towards Finchley Road and attempted to catch his favourite number 13 bus to the West End. A walk around there always relaxed him and would take his mind off things for a while. However, the London Transport bus conductors were not playing ball. They claimed to be too full, even when disgorging ten passengers at his chosen stop. *No room. Up yours. Ding ding.*

He abandoned the idea and walked onwards to the library. This turned out to be busy with all the north Londoners who had missed their bus.

Nelson made his way back to the reference section and obtained the same encyclopaedia he had leafed through a day earlier to discover the letter from NASA.

He opened the book again to the same pages.

"Nothing," sighed Nelson despondently.

"You think you've got problems," said an unemployed bus driver, who had watched him since he entered the room.

Nelson ignored him and stared furiously at the encyclopaedia, finally taking a pincer grip to shake it by the corner, hoping a piece of microdot film might fall to the floor and send him reeling into a world of intrigue, espionage and James Bond girls. His hands perspired and their grasp slipped, dropping the encyclopaedia[16] to a resounding clunk.

"*Pah!*" spat the bus driver.

Nelson leaned over and retrieved his book from the floor. As he did so the pages fell open to reveal a chapter headed *Early Computing*.

It covered the first years, and an announcement in 1948 of the *point-contact transistor* by Bardeen and Brattain, and later the *junction transistor* by Wallace, Sparks and Schockley, and touched on the world's oldest working computer from 1950 in Harwell.

All of these were useful details for his current assignment, but Nelson was aghast. Scrawled across this brief history lesson in thick red ink were the words:

LIES! DAMNED LIES!

From previous journalistic research Nelson knew this coverage to be broadly accurate and so he was bewildered by the apparent anger in the graffiti and why it so vehemently opposed these facts.

An instinct made him take out the letter and reexamine the signature. Grimaldi had signed himself *Dr. Grimaldi*. Though Nelson was no graphologist he could see a distinctive curl of the D in *Dr.* matched with the D in

---

[16] A microdot did fall off, but Nelson didn't notice and hence it was lost forever.

DAMNED.

He looked at the inside front cover of the encyclopaedia. This particular edition has been reprinted in 1967 - a surprisingly old reference book, but a few years before Grimaldi's apparent death. Nelson pondered what it all meant... and whether he should he care.

He flicked through the book, but it gave no more clues, so he replaced it next to a copy of the swimwear edition of Sports Illustrated, a rare find in Swiss Cottage. Nelson distracted himself for the next five minutes, replaced the magazine and stood to leave.

He closed the glass door of the reference section to the sound of a large, flatulent sounding raspberry being blown from the unemployed bus driver's lips.

Nelson froze as two women in the *Hobbies* section he now approached stared at him knowingly. He blushed profusely, stared at the floor and left the library very quickly.

As he walked along Finchley Road back towards West Hampstead his mind raced.

Was something dastardly afoot? Could NASA, the UK government or US government be in on it? Could he get back to see the girl in the towel? Was she in on it? He hoped so. This was exciting, but was it real, and how could he begin to find out? He would telephone NASA.

Call NASA!

Yes, he would make a call to NASA. He would present the name Grimaldi alongside that of Apollo 11, toy with the notion of forty-year delays and add a few dramatic pauses.

And did it stand a chance?

Nelson hurried back to his apartment, unaware of his surroundings and his thoughts in turmoil.

How do you begin to call NASA?

International Directory Enquiries came to mind.

Where is Cape Kennedy, or is it Canaveral? Is NASA still located there because they always talk about Houston having the problem?

His head had once been full of facts about 60's and 70's rockets, astronauts and missions, but it was dawning on Nelson that the last two years of Space Shuttle launches were passing him by. An awareness they mostly landed in the Californian desert was the peak of his familiarity.

Two and a half hours later he was speaking to a switchboard supervisor somewhere in the United States, via British Telecom who had eagerly passed him on.

"Are you still there?" everyone had asked.

"Barely," Nelson had replied.

"We're still trying."

"Yes, you are."

And then unexpectedly, "Will the Public Relations department be sufficient?"

"Yes! Yes please."

"Connecting you. Have a nice day."

After ten purrs the line was opened, and he heard a female voice.

"Hello," it said in a strong Texan drawl. "This is NASA, can I help you?"

Nelson was momentarily stunned the answer had come so calmly, stating he was through to NASA.

"Certainly…" he said recomposing himself, clearing his throat and adopting a charming English accent.

"… certainly you can my dear. Could you kindly tell me if you have a J. Schuger working there as Chief Scientific Officer?" he said, checking the signature on the bottom the recovered letter.

"I'm sorry, but our CSO is not called Schuger. Who wants to know?"

"This is Nelson Staff speaking. Well could you please tell…"

"Oh, hi Nelson. My name is Betty Ann Glaser. You've got a gorgeous accent Nelson."

"So have you," Nelson lied. "Now could you..."

"Should I call you Lord Nelson? We don't get many calls from England. I get excited when we do you know. I think England is a beautiful country. I am a real Anglophile. I adore Stratford-Upon-Avion."

"Avon."

"I beg your pardon."

"Avon. It's Stratford-Upon-Avon."

"Oh yeah. Avon. Ding dong," giggled Betty Ann, "Stratford-Upon-Avon."

"Indeed. Could you..."

"And Convent Garden was the most delightful..."

"No, that's Covent Garden. There are no nuns in it." said Nelson.

"Nuneaton? Oh yeah, I've heard about that as well. Gateway to the South."

"No, that's Balham."

"Sorry?"

"Look, it doesn't matter. All I want to know..."

"You English are so quaint Lord Nelson. Would you like a pen pal?"

"What? No!"

"Why not Nelson?"

"Look, I had one in Tibet who couldn't write," Nelson lied again. He had to stop her. The call was costing him a fortune and this stupid...

"You had a pen pal who couldn't write?" she drawled, "It must have been a bit of a one-sided conversation."

Nelson was sinking deeper.

"Look, will you just tell me where I can contact Mr. Schuger."

"Just a minute Nelson. Sorry, *Schuger* you said? Ah. I'm sorry but I am not at liberty to divulge that information," replied Betty Ann, abruptly adopting a bureaucratic position.

"Then please could you put me through to someone who is!"

"Only if we swap addresses."

Nelson gave up and told her his address, without the strength to make one up.

"Okay," she said, "If your request is for Schuger I will put you through to Mr. Franks. He's the boss most of the time. Don't forget to write dear Lord."

Nelson took the phone from his hot ear and rubbed it as a relief. Yet another pause followed.

"Hello, Mr Staff is it?" said another voice finally.

"Yes."

"Good, I hope I've got that right. This is Mr. Franks, Head of Corporate Affairs. Now, what is it we can do for you?"

"Well," began Nelson, "I would like to know if you have, or ever had, a Mr. J. Schuger working as your Chief Scientific Officer?"

There was a long pause - too long.

"Er, *Schuger*… you knew Mr. Schuger did you?" came the careful reply.

"Then he did work for NASA then?"

"…no, I didn't say…"

"And he's dead now? Or did he leave?"

Nelson heard the mouthpiece of Mr. Frank's telephone being covered followed by muted instructions. If he had doubt before, he was now confident that something very strange was going on.

"Yes, I'm afraid he's dead now," came the final answer, "You knew him, did you?"

"Not really, but I have a letter here of his… to Doctor Oscar Grimaldi."

"Oh… oh, really? Staff you said?"

"No, Grimaldi."

"No, I mean that you said your name was Staff."

"Yes."

"And your address?"

"Your secretary has all the details, unfortunately."

Nelson suddenly experienced a cold tremor that he had given his real address. What on God's Earth did he think he was doing? But it was too late to stop himself.

"Why was the Apollo 11 landing forty years late?" demanded Nelson.

There was a cough followed by a dull thud and rattle via satellite. A moment later the telephone was picked up and another voice spoke. This was a deep guttural voice unlike the softer voice of Mr. Franks. It said:

"We'll be in touch Mr. Nelson Staff."

Click, purr.

CHAPTER 16

Zen slept as Cha'3E took is seat and unfolded his GlasSlate® phablet. One half of his transparent screen instantly clouded to display the remaining agenda of their meeting. A bullet point displayed a live news feed scrolling the latest on UFO sightings in the local area. He was not overly concerned but it was coverage they needed to minimize. Although lengthy, the timeline for *The Quit* was still on schedule.

The huge, frosted door to the meeting room opened abruptly and two tall figures in grey robes rushed in.

"The room is in use!"

"Our apologies 3E, but it is urgent," stuttered the slightly taller, paler of the two.

"What is it?"

"There has been a breach."

"From where!"

"The *surface*."

"Exactly where on the *surface*?"

"England. London," he then took a deep breath, "NW6 3DZ."

"West Hampstead!"

"I'm afraid so."

"*No!*" He slammed the conference table. "What happened?"

"He called NASA… and got through."

"*What*? Okay, understood. This has to be the last of it. You…" he indicated to the slightly shorter on in grey robes, "…get me 6M on the vidcon."

"And you… keep talking. I want to know all about who *he* is. I'm going to finish it personally this time."

CHAPTER 17

Moments after his call Nelson was elated. He grinned, pursed his lips and nodded. His chest puffed slightly, and he caught sight of himself in the bathroom mirror. He could not recall any famous painting having this degree of smugness captured within it.

He had ruffled NASA's feathers. He reminisced on his boyhood awe of the organisation. 2:56 a.m. GMT on the 21st July 1969: Neil Armstrong first set foot on the Moon. Recognising the passion in her son, his Mum had presented Nelson with a beautifully detailed pop-up book describing the mission. He took himself back to the fuzzy TV images in black and white - and he remembered vividly Armstrong's words when he step out of the lunar landing module and made the first footprint on the Moon's surface: "One small step for man, one giant leap for mankind."

He had gaped intently at Armstrong on his television and thought:

I bet he feels great.

His pop-up book had revealed the Americans laid out an estimated six billion dollars in 1960s money to get Armstrong, Aldrin and Collins to the Moon. Nelson was satisfied his one telephone call had achieved a similar feeling of self-satisfaction - for far less expense.

Then the cold tremor hit him again, followed swiftly by the self-doubt.

What was he doing?

He was evidently bored, and in need of excitement. But why had he given his real address?

That evening Nelson rummaged through his

fridge in search of an elusive block of cheddar. He settled on a yoghurt just two days beyond its sell-by date, deciding it was both safe and inescapable. He stood at the living room window staring at the road below flooded yellow by streetlamps. He picked at the carton with a teaspoon and between mouthfuls of Waitrose peach melba flavour his lips were pursed again. He caught his reflection in the glass and smiled at this image of smugness.

He then noticed a shadowy figure walking past in the street carrying a rucksack and long lens SLR camera. Strangely, the figure turned to point the camera at him. Nelson flinched as a huge flash illuminated his face.

"Funny," he thought, "perhaps it's an artist."

He was wrong.

CHAPTER 18

1983

1st September
11:45am CST, Houston TX

Tan'6M sat in his car at the Johnson Space Center. He took the precaution of parking in a far corner bay, reversing tight to the manicured hedgerow. No colleague could approach him without being seen. Though it was a very warm day his windows remained closed, the engine running, and the air conditioning on low. He opened his briefcase, sifted through his papers, Filofax, partially melted Summit bar, and printed agendas forming the rest of his day. He found the tiny catch to release its secret compartment. He took out the GlasSlate® mobile phone, unfolded its slim crystal plates and tapped the vidcon icon.

He saw the conference had already started and clicked *Join*. The only face to appear was that of Cha'3E, who he greeted in his usual rasping voice.

"Hello Cha, good to see you again."

Silence.

"You're on mute, Cha."

Bip.

"...*hell*! I'm gonna need a T-shirt made for me with that printed on it. Can you hear me now?"

"Sure."

"How are you Tan?"

"I'm good thanks Cha. How's *The Quit* progressing?"

"The funding plans are falling into place. And we got the big reply. So, we're all on schedule… except for this potential blip."

"How much do you know already?"

"Just a few basics. Go from the top."

"Okay. It came through first thing this morning, our time. Since the last breach I set up a procedure if anyone mentions Shu's old name, they are routed through to me. He spoke to switchboard and my colleague Franks. They did their job but remain oblivious."

"Good. Well done."

"He was calling from West Hampstead and seemed to know quite a lot."

"What do we know about *him*?"

"A fair amount so far, even though he obviously leaves no digital dust. How much do you want to know?"

"All of it please Tan. We've just taken the rare decision to *erase* him. And I'm going to take personal charge."

CHAPTER 19

1983. One day later.

Nelson awoke to the pitter patter of the same DJ talking about his fellow DJs, and then which DJs would be hosting which shows throughout the DJ day. The teasmaid created another pot of steaming hot Darjeeling ready to be poured.

He yawned, realising no shocking revelations had transpired since sundown, and no mysterious voices had reached out.

He rolled over in bed and got out, showered, dressed, considered life on a cosmic scale and decided he was low on toilet roll.

The clear weather had given way to September rain. The supermarket was very crowded, and Waitrose provides its shoppers with the option of heavy wire baskets or large, four wheeled trollies. His survival instinct urged Nelson to acquire the last trolley in the rack.

Inevitably it had just three good wheels, and adamantly tugged him relentlessly into the baked beans, dried spices and peach melba yoghurts. Nelson noted a lone trolley in the supermarket not squeaking or wrestling being pushed by someone who appeared dimly familiar.

He completed his shopping, sustaining just one bruised thigh and a minor scrape of the Achilles tendon. He made his way to the checkout and the ritual of being displaced by the north London ladies with one box of tea or a bag of grapes. *(You don't mind do you.)* He filed into the shortest queue - which took three times longer to clear than any other - and stood yearning for the checkout girl to smile.

At that moment, as he prepared to argue over forfeiting the small fee for a large carrier bag advertising the supermarket's brand, he was distracted by the same person in command of the faithful trolley.

Nelson reluctantly paid his bill, having left it too late to complain whilst the checkout girl shouted for Maureen to take over her shift and change the till roll. On his way out he passed the same individual once more who was busy packing away her own shopping.

It was a girl - so far so good - and she looked vaguely familiar. She was evidently intelligent - packing groceries into old carrier bags she had remembered to bring with her. But Nelson was not studying her brains.

In Nelson's opinion, she had nice legs.

She was vaguely familiar, and she had nice legs.

Surely... he was better than this?

A mind reader walked past in the street and frowned at Nelson.

Nelson recomposed himself, sighed, and carried on his way from the store. The rain had stopped, and it left gleaming pavements with the sense of a cooler autumn day. As he walked, the girl overtook him outside. Suddenly a word sprang into his mind.

"Towel!" said Nelson, and he unexpectedly recalled who she was.

She walked in front of him for a little while longer. Her brunette hair touched the pulled-up collar of a grey raincoat complemented by dark red court shoes. Her heels clicked on the pavement as Nelson scurried along - nearly dropping his soap powder in the process. He increased his pace and plucked up the courage.

"Remember me?" he heard himself saying.

The girl turned sharply, slowed and stared at him.

"No," she said abruptly, sweeping strands of hair from her face with her free hand.

"Yesterday. Halfway through your shower and the doorbell rang."

"Oh yes," she said, her brown eyes widening in concern.

"I'm sorry about that, about the mix-up."

"Good," she said, and a thin smile appeared on her face.

"Now if you'll..."

A colossal eighteen-wheel, articulated lorry slid to a sudden halt beside them, its air brakes hissing madly. Four large men leapt out of the back dressed in black jeans and windcheater jackets. They had Nelson and the girl clearly in their sights. The driver jumped from the front cab, clicking madly with his large camera and flash. Nelson and the girl were collected by two men each and incredibly swiftly bundled into the back of the lorry with loud shouts and strong kicks from her, and just one scream from Nelson. Groceries flew, Nelson dropped his soap powder, and it was kicked along the pavement leaving a bluey-whiteness in its trail. The camera stopped clicking and flashing and the driver climbed back into his cab. The lorry blew its horn and left, smoothly disappearing as fast as it had arrived.

Finchley Road pedestrians glanced around for evidence of hidden TV crews.

Inside the lorry's trailer the girl maintained her yelling.

"No! NO! Get off *me*! Help! *Police*! Who the... HELP!"

She and Nelson were swiftly and professionally tied up and left together in a corner where sunlight poured in through a small skylight. The girl kicked and shouted and screamed. Her best volley had connected with her attacker's shins yet caused little reaction.

"Love, we're not here to hurt ya," was all the man

built like a bear would say.

Her neck and cheeks flushed red, she was breathing too fast and stared fiercely at Nelson.

"Who... ARE *YOU*?" she screamed.

"I'm sorry..." started Nelson.

"STOP! Look Mister..." she hissed, "if this is some kind of weird abduction thing you can just f..."

"N... no!" stuttered Nelson, "honest."

He took in the trailer's interior, noticing it gleamed improbably white with newness and cleanliness. It was spotless, save for a couple of Coca Cola cans dropped on the floor and what appeared to be an empty sandwich packet. The ceiling glowed from a hidden light source.

He glanced at his captors who were nonchalantly huddled in the far corner, now preoccupied with a group activity.

"*Who are you!*" he cried towards them.

One looked indifferently over his shoulder and then returned to focus on his cohorts.

"Who *ARE* you!" shrieked Nelson. There was still no response. And Nelson wasn't really expecting one. He suspected he knew who these people were, or at least who they were connected to.

The girl stared fixedly at Nelson.

"*HELP!*"

And then, "Get *me* out of here..." the words left hanging in the air.

Further moments passed with an unnerving quiet. The girl's stare unsettled Nelson, but what worried him the most was his sudden need to break wind. Finally, she cracked before he did.

"Who the hell are you?" she hissed.

"Nelson, Nelson Staff. No relation. I'm very sorry about all..."

"To whom?"

"I'm sorry?"

"No relation to whom?"

"President Vic. Vic the Vegan. Vic Staff, the Vegas Vegan."

Nelson saw the girl start to shiver. He struggled to determine if it was due to the cold, shock or hysteria.

"Don't worry," tried Nelson, "I realise that this may seem like the weirdest thing to happen as you leave Waitrose."

The girl stopped her shivering when she noticed the look on Nelson's face as he studied her raincoat, and she cursed her own slack preparation for the morning's shopping.

"What's your name?" he asked.

"Tina Reagan. No relation."

"To whom?"

"The Leader of the Free World? President... forget it," said Tina, and shivered again.

A quiet moment passed and Nelson studied the interior of the trailer, observing a nearby side door in addition to the rear swing doors through which they were bundled. This anterior door appeared to be sealed with a glistening, black substance applied to cover the whole frame. It also housed an unused *Push-Bar-To-Open* handle.

"Anyway," said Nelson, "don't worry. I think we'll be fine."

"*We*? I do not care one toss about you. Just get me out."

The silence returned again for a few moments then she leaned forward and said much quieter: "Ok. Where the hell are we, and who are these gorillas?"

"Mister Grumpy, Mister Snorty, Mister Meany..." started Nelson.

"For someone who doesn't have a clue you seem to be taking all of this very jovially."

"I make jokes when I'm nervous, sorry. I honestly don't know who they are, but I do think that we are on our way to America."

"Where!"

"America. Cape Kennedy to be more precise. Or is it Canaveral?"

"Cape Canaveral?" challenged Tina.

"I think so," and then after a pause Nelson said, "It could be worse."

"How?"

"We could be on our way back home."

"Is that a joke?"

"No."

Tina was one of the many unhappy children of Margaret Thatcher's United Kingdom. She graduated from a redbrick university two years earlier. As unemployment reached three million, she had moved to London. In place of fame and fortune, she took the only job she could find as PA to the owner of a small estate agency. The housing market was contracting and consolidating, and with interest rates stuck at ten percent, her employer's revenue slowly dried up. He had *regretfully* made her redundant just one week earlier. With her bubble burst, she was lucky to get two months redundancy pay, which is the amount of time Tina was giving herself before returning to her parent's northern town.

Something had to turn up.

Although she professed not to understand Nelson's remark, as it sank in the words began to ring true.

She did not know quite what to make of this person before her with his friendly, green-grey eyes and innocent smile.

Their abduction was clear, yet he seemed certain they were not in grave danger. Was he insane, or just very calm?

Or was he in on this?   How could she open the chocolate Digestive biscuits in her shopping bag with her hands tied?

Tina felt her shivering worsen.

"Are you cold?" asked Nelson.

"No," she lied, "Didn't you say that you were going to get us out of here?"

"Did I?"

"Yes."

"Did it sound good?"

"Sort of."

"Oh good."

"Well, are you?"

"Am I what?"

"Are you going to get us out of here?"

"Well, not exactly."

"Don't you *want* to get out?   I mean, we have been abducted, haven't we?"

"Yes, I believe that is the correct term, but I don't actually want to escape, not at the moment," admitted Nelson, as much to himself as to Tina. He then tried to get up but failed miserably having overlooked his legs were tied together.

"Why? Why don't you want to escape?" ask Tina trying to understand more.

"Because we are on our way to the Cape. Haven't you always wanted to go to America?"

"Not this way."

"NASA wants to see me. I think," added Nelson.

"NASA. *You*! Ha!"

"There's no need to be…"

"I'm sorry," said Tina, "but I fail to see why NASA would go to all this trouble to pick you up in such a dramatic way. Now I am really worried. It's not NASA –

they don't do this sort of stuff. And why am I here anyway?"

"Well, the last point I'm not too sure about either. It could be that you were an innocent bystander."

"*What!*" hissed Tina. "I've told you, if this is some weird pick-up routine, I'll be kicking your…"

"It isn't a pick-up routine, I promise," interrupted Nelson, trying desperately and ungainly to get to his feet. He began to hop his way over to their four captors.

"So… we're not escaping?" called Tina after him.

"Ssshh! No," he hissed. A few more hops and then he flopped down beside the huge gorillas who he now observed were playing cards.

"Hello," called Nelson in the general direction of the granite faces.

Silence.

"Gin," said one of them finally.

"Yes please," said Nelson, "any tonic?"

Four heads turned slowly, as if mounted on huge gears. They stared at Nelson with coldness and contempt in their eyes.

"Sorry, I thought you meant a drink. I say things like that when I'm nervous," pleaded Nelson to the gorilla who had just laid down seven cards.

The heads turned away again and went back to their game. One started shuffling the cards. He then dealt quickly in silence.

"Will we be flying to Cape Canaveral?" tried Nelson as the last card was laid out.

Just one of them looked at him with the same cold stare. Abruptly, he burst out laughing. He folded his cards into his giant hand and said:

"Did tha' hear 'im. Is 'e thick? Our mate here reckons he's flyin' t'America."

The others smiled to each other and then another turned to Nelson.

"Get back wi ya. Tha'll have t'make do wi'

Yorkshire."

"Yorkshire!" exclaimed Nelson, checking the faces of all four in turn. "*Yorkshire!*"

The one who had laughed put his cards down, stood up and lifted Nelson with ease by his ropes and dragged him back to the far end of the trailer. He unceremoniously dumped him next to Tina and returned to his game.

Nelson remained there, winded and bruised. As he lay, Tina tapped him on the head with her shoe.

"You were saying?" she said.

"I was saying… we have to escape."

Nelson rolled over and sat up.

"Yes indeed, that's what you were saying," she said.

Another three uneventful hours ticked by. The trailer's wheels rolling on motorway roads became the main soundtrack with sporadic overtaking engine clatter passing them by. Nelson noted the apparent lack of noise from the truck's engines, only a monotonous whirring, as if fueled similar to a colossal electric milk float.

He tried one more discourse with the gorillas. This met with silence and a hasty drag back to his original resting place.

Towards the front of the trailer, away from the gorillas, Nelson now stood against the sealed door that had piqued his interest earlier. Tina sat nearby, staring fixedly away from Nelson. Due to a combination of fatigue and despondency she had agreed to his request of distractedly humming, sometimes singing, none of it particularly tuneful.

In the last few minutes, a bizarre sequence of thoughts had sped through Nelson's mind.

Was Yorkshire their genuine destination? Could that possibly be compatible with any NASA connection? Tina has amazing eyes and wonderful legs. Grow up! If not NASA, why the abduction? Coke Is It! Not to my taste, too sugary. Who do they really want? An empty Coca Cola can. Those legs. For God's sake man, you are pathetic. Am I an innocent bystander? Is Tina the target? This shimmering door sealant and a can of Coke. What have I got myself into? I can tear that can in half. Perhaps I should escape, but how? Coke Is It! Gimme Gimme Gimme A Man After Midnight. The black sealant… tear the can in half.

This cerebral drivel led Nelson to be standing against the sealed door, his tied hands still behind his back, gouging large chunks of the black sealant using the torn edge of a Coca-Cola can.[17]

Tina's role was to slowly ease the can towards Nelson with her feet, and then sing. Nelson claimed back spasm and the need to stand. Luckily the four gorillas were so involved in their card game they paid him little attention.

Another hour of toil made the clearance job as good as possible, but any high reach was hampered by his ties. He whispered this concern to Tina.

"Well, if you kick it hard enough it should open anyway," she said quietly.

"Are you any good at untying knots?" he asked.

"No."

"Me neither, but these ropes around my feet have loosened in the last few hours. Try pulling them."

Nelson sat down on the floor with his feet behind Tina's back, near her hands. She began pulling at what ropes she could reach with her fingers.

The ropes began to ease, and Nelson felt he could

---

[17] Why the ABBA lyrics came in remains a mystery.

remove a leg from his bindings. Before he pulled it completely free, he moved over to attempt the same with Tina's cords.

This took longer and much fiddling, but after many minutes of cramped and sore fingers, Tina's ropes were almost free.

Nelson sensed the lorry gradually reduce speed. A few moments later it rocked to a halt, and its air brakes hissed. Two of their captors stood up to check the situation. They approached the rear double doors – away from Nelson and Tina.

"This could be our chance!" breathed Nelson, as he watched their captors move away. It was a long trailer, and there were at least ten to fifteen paces between them.

Nelson shook off the rest of the ropes around his feet and indicated to Tina to do the same. Both still had their hands bound behind their backs.

"This *is* our chance," roared Nelson, his adrenalin flowing freely. He had never been in such a situation throughout his entire life – and now he was going to escape in a most spectacular manner. He was eager to kick down that door with all his focused strength and intensity, leap onto the motorway embankment followed by a pretty girl, perform a tumble roll (even though his hands were tied), and then career down the hard shoulder weaving and screaming between passing motorists, forcing them to stop. He was going to set them free with flair and panache.

"Er, Nelson…" said Tina, watching the far end of the trailer.

But Nelson was high, and he ignored her. If their captors had noticed his intentions, they could never react before his lightning reflexes kicked open this door and he whisked Tina from danger.

"Nelson…" she tried again.

But his mind was made up. He remained laser focused – with only one crazed ambition.

He stepped back.

The adrenalin pumped.

"Er, Nelson…"

The blood surged.

He raised his right leg, the muscles tensed, Nelson heaved…

CRASH!

The door splintered from its sealant and burst open.

Nelson prepared to jump out. He was ready to leap out onto… the clinically clean, white-tiled, floor of an immensely curved corridor?

"Well done Mr. Staff," said the man in a U.S. Air Force uniform, "we've been trying to get that door sorted since we took delivery of the truck."

"Nelson…" said Tina, still transfixed on the far end of the trailer. The main rear doors had been opened.

"…I think we've arrived."

She pointed to the opening revealing further evidence of the lengthy, dazzling white tunnel stretching into the distance behind.

"Yes ma'am, you sure have," confirmed the U.S.A.F officer. He spoke from his vantage point below them as he stared up through the small, renovated emergency exit, vestiges of its black sealant still clinging to the frame.

Nelson wept.

CHAPTER 20

"Pull yourself together Nelson," said Tina as she helped him down from the eighteen-wheeler.

"I'm sure he'll be fine," said the American, "Follow me please."

Nelson picked his head up and looked around. The long white tunnel stretched behind them, curving slightly such that it obscured any entrance. There was a long white tunnel in front that curved to a similar degree so that no exit was visible either. The only detail observable in this gleaming arc was the precise tiles and grouting of the walls.

"What is this?" asked Nelson, "some kind of..."

"All will become clear," said the American, "I hope," he added under his breath. He continued.

"I'm Chief Master Sergeant W. J. McGuigan of the Progressionary Unit US Air Force, seconded as a Senior NCO to assist in *The Quit*."

"Well, that's much clearer now," said Nelson.

"But you can call me Whip."

"Must we?" derided Nelson as he looked at Tina. She appeared to have now accepted this change to her daily routine and he sensed she was dealing with it much better than him. His expectations of NASA freely involved private jet extraction, guided tours of the new Space Shuttles, his hushed name on everyone's lips, even a complimentary NASA T-shirt and baseball cap. He had allowed himself a delusional flight of fancy where he called the shots. It was a flight completely detached from the reality of any outward threat or menace. He permitted himself to feel in safe hands with NASA.

He did not feel safe now.

"Where are we?" he asked.

"Yorkshire," came the reply.

"Where in Yorkshire?" asked Tina.

"Underneath it."

"Oh."

"Beneath the Peak District to be precise. Follow me," came the command again.

Nelson walked beside Tina as they both followed W. J. McGuigan. More troubled thoughts passed through his mind.

What was an American nicknamed Whip in an Air Force uniform planning beneath Yorkshire? Why were they surrounded by white tiles? And what was he, Nelson, doing following the American... and three elderly men dressed in red robes, each gliding on a strange two-wheeled device with a long stem projecting from its base-plate?

"Don't look round yet..." hissed Tina under her breath.

"I've seen them," whispered Nelson.

"Then we're both crazy."

The floating vehicles' stem finished with a handlebar that the three old men lightly gripped.

The scene had confronted Nelson and Tina as they rounded the front of the truck. Nelson now turned to observe directly. He knew strong, white light could play tricks. Abruptly one of the of gorilla guards pushed him hard in the shoulder to deflect his attention.

No one spoke for at least a minute. Finally, the three elderly companions simultaneously leaned forward very slightly on their handlebars and casually slid past them on the two-wheeled device with no visible means of balance. The whole contraption seemed to defy any laws of physics.

"Now *that*... is a mode of transport I like the look of," said Nelson. "Do you get a lot of these?" he asked flatly.

"Yessir," said W. J McGuigan, almost as a salute. "It's called a Segway."

"A... a Segg Weigh... or a segue? Like a

131

transition?"

"Yessir, great implementation of gyroscopics."

"Hmm…" said Nelson, not sure he was understanding, "…and what about the men in robes riding these Segg Weighs?"

"They are the Knowalls."

"The Knowalls…" repeated Nelson.

"Yessir."

"Mr. and Mrs. Knowall and their son Benny?"

"No. It refers to knowledge, technology and stuff like that."

"Oh, the Know-*Alls*," said Nelson, "very original."

"Yessir."

Tina checked around to see they were flanked by two of the impassive gorillas and saw the truck being removed behind them. She and Nelson then followed their red-robed companions silently for a few minutes. The only faint sound came from each two-wheeled Segway, invisible motors rolling smoothly and balancing incomprehensibly before them.

No sign of an entrance or exit in the tiling had yet to reveal itself. They were clearly in a strange place. Nelson glanced thoughtfully at Tina.

The Knowalls? Knowledge, technology and stuff like that? What did that mean?

Nelson then felt compelled to ask something that had disturbed him the last half hour or so. It was pressing, but true espionage dreams were not rendered with questions such as this.

"Is there a toilet near here?" he said finally, when he could no longer wait.

Nelson relieved himself in a white cubicle, the door of which had effortlessly lifted as one of the

Knowalls stared at it. Everyone politely turned away for Nelson and the cistern flushed automatically as he pulled up his zip. The journey continued with an uncomfortable silence.

Finally, they arrived at an immense gold and copper door that terminated the curved tunnel.

The heavy portal slid open on impressively robust hinges to reveal a gigantic chamber, perfectly hemispherical in structure, its roof entirely coated by a myriad of flickering lights.

In the far distance a small spotlight picked out a female of striking blond hair, a lustrous white robe, finished with brilliant white boots. She also stood on a Segway. Two of their red-robed companions separated from the group to wordlessly join her. The third smiled enigmatically and stayed with Nelson, Tina and the uniformed American.

"Sit down please," invited Sergeant McGuigan.

He pointed to an isolated black bench centered on a dark floor stretching in all directions towards the distant shadows. Nelson and Tina obliged and sat in awe of the marvel above them. Gazing starry eyed around the chamber they became aware of the same soft, mechanical whirring. The Knowalls resting on their Segways in the darkness, leaned forward and rolled away to disappear through a separate exit, together with their female colleague. Her spotlight faded away.

"Who's the companion?" she asked, as the exit closed behind them to reseal a wall of black.

The Knowall who waited in the chamber stepped from his Segway. It rocked faintly, but somehow remained perfectly balanced. Tina noticed the thin gold braid that ran across his red robe from shoulder to torso was embellished with a cloud motif. He was shaven headed but with a thick white-stubble beard. His hazel eyes had a warmness to them.

"Mr. Nelson Staff," he said to them both, more as a statement than a question.

"Yes," replied Nelson, leaning forward.

"Ah you. Okay, and who might this be? We have no evidence of a wife or girlfriend."

"This is Tina. I met her yesterday."

"Tina Reagan," added Tina, "no relation."

"To whom?" asked the Knowall.

"Forget it."

Chief Master Sergeant W. J McGuigan ordered the two gorillas to follow him, returning to the huge metal entrance door. It began to close as silently as it had opened and he turned to perform an efficient salute towards the room. He disappeared, accompanied by a distant hiss as the chamber was resealed.

This left Nelson, Tina, the Knowall and a hundred thousand twinkling lights. Without command, two more objects rose from the floor to break the monotony of the darkness - a small keyboard plinth and the thinnest, flattest TV screen Nelson had ever seen.

Nelson's gaped at the TV and then the chamber roof, as the Knowall shuffled to arrange his robe and smooth his golden clouds. The ceiling was beautiful and unbelievable. Part of it - he thought - reminded Nelson of the constellation of Orion[18].

"Where are we?"

"Yorkshire," replied the Knowall.

---

[18] One possible explanation could be the small collection of lights on which Nelson focused formed an exact copy of the constellation of Orion. In fact, though he would not perceive this, the roof depicted an accurate representation of the night sky as viewed from the county of Yorkshire, and was rotating imperceptibly as the hours wore on. Another section of the ceiling reminded Nelson of a Christmas decoration he purchased the previous year. This has no explanation.

"Yes, yes, I know all that. The Peak District, and beneath it. Is this part of NASA?"

"No," the old man told him, "but you could say that NASA was part of us... couldn't you?"

"Sorry?"

"Hmm..." pondered the Knowall, his piercing hazel eyes drilling into Nelson.

"Why are we here?" asked Nelson as the stare began to unnerve him.

"I thought you knew that?" came the response.

"Do I?"

"Hmm... Do you like change, Nelson Staff?"

"What? Well, I prefer larger notes really, but big coins are fine."

"No, I mean real change... transformation. Revolution. Do you like change for change's sake?"

"What?"

"Great place for a disco," interrupted Tina.

Nelson recognized the Knowall was performing some sort of assessment with his unflinching gaze. Nelson squirmed in his seat and broke eye contact many times. A quiet tension began to mount in the room. Finally, the Knowall relented and turned to smile at Tina.

"And you my dear, is it true you've only just met Nelson?"

"I wouldn't even say I've met him. He knocked on my door yesterday and then chased me from the supermarket today."

"That's not fair, not fair," sighed Nelson.

"But if I get your question correctly," continued Tina, "I love change. I always have. It makes things a bit more... exciting."

The Knowall contemplated this statement whilst looking once more between them both and appeared to have reached a decision.

"Hmm..." he concluded, "so we will *erase* you after all."

"Erase?" gasped Nelson. Tina snapped her head to look at him and then back at the Knowall.

"Why of course," replied the old man.

"How do you mean... *erase*?"

"All will become clear," he said as he turned to leave the chamber. He headed for the same exit through which his colleagues had disappeared. Just before the door closed, he turned and smiled.

"Are you wearing anything under that raincoat?" he asked Tina as the door hissed shut.

Tina looked blankly at the closed door and then down at the floor.

"Erased..." she exhaled. "Just *what* have you got me into?"

"Sorry Tina, I'm no longer sure."

She turned her back on Nelson and the artificial stars above them twinkled.

Nelson stared at the stars. Tina stared at the floor. A stillness had descended on the chamber and neither of them moved. Their anxiety levels were rising, but neither would speak first to admit it. As he stared at the lights above him Nelson could see a twitching beneath Orion's belt. A tiny square of the ceiling folded in on itself, and a small close-circuit television camera began to appear.

"Look," he indicated.

"Oh my God!" spat Tina, "If this is Candid Camera..."

"Jesus, no..." said Nelson, but then smiling self-consciously at the lens, "... do you think this is my best side?"

"I'm asking again, what the *hell* am I doing here?"

"I'm not sure."

"Not sure. *Not sure*! You must have some idea.

The only thing I know is that there is £14.79's worth of shopping scattered over Finchley Road and a day out that I'd planned is completely... completely... ruined!"

Nelson awkwardly stretched his neck from side to side and linked his fingers.

"*Well*?" demanded Tina.

He swiveled on the bench to face her directly.

"Okay, a very long story, short. I write articles when I can. Technical ones for magazines and newspapers. These aren't in the slightest bit technical - which suites me fine because neither am I. The editors seem to think that I have a simple way of explaining and talking down to the readership, but if I'm honest it's because I haven't got a clue half the time what I'm writing about. You've heard of the ZX81 or Commodore 64 I presume?"

Tina nodded.

"So, because these are gaining a toehold, one of the Sunday supplements commissions me to write an article on them and link it to the history of computers. So far so good. The newspaper demands an angle to say they will never take off. I could agree. Why would any normal person need a computer in their home!

I start the assignment and soon realise it's going to take a lot longer that I estimated. I'm tidying up one section and find myself digging around resources in the local library. Then... there's this letter in a reference book that probably hasn't been opened for years. It's from NASA to a Doctor Grimaldi - who used to live where you live now. That... is why I came to your place."

"And got me out of the shower. Okay, go on."

"I'm so sorry about that. The letter talks about Grimaldi's opinions on rocket fuel for the forthcoming Moon landing. But, what's *so* weird is that the letter's date... get this, 1927. Not written once, twice. That's over forty years before Neil Armstrong lets us know how smug you can be as the first one up there. What do you do, ignore it as a fake? I tried to return it to you, big failure as we both know. I went back to the library, and then find *Lies All Lies* scrawled across pages about inventions leading to the first computers. If it is a fake, then they're going to a lot of effort, and in the most obscure places. So, the wind in my sails I ring NASA and a whimpering brain cell has trouble breathing when I mention Grimaldi and Moon in the same sentence, and then a voice that should be advertising aftershave says *We'll be in touch*. And here I am."

And me? he could see Tina saying by splaying hands.

"And… I think you're here because you've got nice legs."

Tina slapped Nelson smartly across the face. She held back a scream, but her face reddened.

"That's fair enough," said Nelson, his face smarting, but maintaining eye contact. "I deserved that. I'm *so* sorry, that's all I can say again. I didn't foresee any of this, and you were never part of it."

He turned back on his seat to face the huge door they entered through.

"I got all wrapped up in my head. I'm a true idiot. You've been so calm."

He paused for a moment, and then turned back to Tina.

"We need to find a way out of here," he said finally.

"Out of where? Underneath Yorkshire and this circular tube of white tiling? Fan-bloody-tastic. You look at a map of the world and there's this little flashing dot in the middle of England which says *You Are Here*. Thanks a lot Mr. Knowall. Oh… to be *above* Yorkshire. To be in a 707, first class to JFK, limo to Manhattan, top floor at the Plaza, dinner at…"

"I think you'll find..."

"Shut up. Don't spoil my rant."

"Shall I leave you to it?" said Nelson, rising from the bench.

"What. No! Come back!" yelled Tina, "You've got to listen."

Nelson stood a few steps away from her with a hand on his still smarting cheek. He then relented and reseated himself.

"Moon landings. 1927. NASA. Don't you see Nelson, it's all *Boys Own* conspiracy crap. Straight out of a *Quinn Martin* production. Next thing is you'll start talking about aliens and E bloody T."

"I still haven't seen it yet," said Nelson.

"What!"

"*Phone hooooome…*"

"Get stuffed!" said Tina to the world.

They sat again in silence as Tina cooled off. Choosing his moment and words carefully, Nelson whispered softly.

"So, if we're going to escape - and I really, really want to now, then we need calm, intellect and a brilliant idea."

"We're stuck down here for life then," huffed Tina.

Nelson rose from his seat and moved towards the keyboard and incredulously flat screen that remained in place after the Knowall left the room. He stared at its blankness and noticed a tiny logo etched into its surface that he did not recognise. He ran one finger lightly across the keyboard and saw a switched marked with a small *1* and *0*.

Nelson pressed it.

The screen sprang to life, told him that he was using GlasSlate® OS version 28.7. It briefly informed him a full memory scan was being undertaken to detect any faults, and subsequently a *wireless network* was now being established. Nelson pondered what this could mean as the cursor blinked. Finally, the screen cleared, and a single word appeared at the top.

Yes? it said.

Nelson took the initiative and stood before the keyboard.

Yes what? he typed.

What do you wish to know? was the reply.

It dawned on Nelson what he had at his fingertips. He turned to Tina and whispered.

"What was it the Knowall said he was going to do with us?"

She looked at him with the contempt still clear in her face.

"Erase us," she hissed.

"*Erase*, that was it," said Nelson and proceeded to ask the screen for a definition.

Standard or Revised? it queried.

Revised typed Nelson assuming a more relevant definition would ensue.

The delay was a few seconds but when the screen replied it showed just five words. Nelson's body shot through a cold chill and the colour drained from his face. He felt physically sick.

"Are you okay?" asked Tina watching him suddenly support himself by grabbing the sides of the flat screen.

"I asked... I asked this computer thing for their definition of *erase*."

"And?"

"Look."

Tina rushed to the screen. The five words caused her to gasp. The screen displayed:

Removed from the human race.

Nelson's head snapped in multiple directions as he frantically looked around. He recognised something in the tiny illuminations above, but it must be a quirk of the light. He glanced at the television camera still monitoring their movements. Again he spotted something in the ceiling lights, but assumed he was imagining. He looked at Tina, who was still staring at the screen. He focused back on the lights. The more he stared the more they twinkled and formed into shapes. Did some of them really come together near the artificial horizon to spell the words 'Emergency Exit'? Just above what he had assumed to be a black hole in the map of the cosmos?

Never.

Yes...?

YES!

"Do you think that camera can shoot?"

"What?" asked Tina.

"Never mind. Let's go."

He grabbed hold of her arm and dashed towards the sign.

"What the hell are you doing?"

"This is an emergency, and we need an exit."

"What!"

"Trust me."

Nelson and Tina plunged headlong into the black hole.

CHAPTER 21

Of course, it was not a black hole. No. It was yet another corridor, only this time covered in black tiles fixed with black cement. There were no lights and no reflective surfaces, and though they could not know it, the corridor curved slightly so that they could no longer see the door they ran through or where they were going to. They ran on into the darkness.

"Where are we going?" pleaded Tina.

"This is an emergency exit, which means a way out."

"But… where will it lead?"

"I don't know. Out."

"Oh Nelson," said a voice from nowhere. "Are you really a Luddite?"

"Who was that?" hissed Nelson.

"I don't know, it came from nowhere. And what's a Luddite?" said Tina.

Nelson fumbled to grab Tina's hand in the pitch black and pulled her along with him.

"Keep running."

"Wait, slow down."

"Why?"

"My raincoat has come undone."

"Hell! Why now?"

"I've got an idea," said Tina.

"What, here?" asked Nelson.

"Stare at the wall," said Tina.

"Hmm?"

"Stare at the wall."

"WHAT?"

"Stare… at… the wall."

"Why should I stare at the wall?" Nelson shrieked.

"Don't you remember?"

"No, I don't bleeding well remember."

"When you wanted to relieve yourself in the white tunnel the Knowall stared at the wall and a cubicle appeared. We don't know how long this tunnel is, but from that hollow voice we can guess they know we're in it."

"So?"

"So... I presume there will be someone waiting for us at the end. Stare at the wall and..."

"Hold on, what's all this *Listen to me I'm leader* routine," interrupted Nelson.

"*You* said, in order to escape we needed calm, intellect and a brilliant idea."

"Yes?"

"Well, someone has to provide all three. Stare... at... the wall."

"What wall?"

"That one."

"But I can't even see it. I can't even remember if my eyes are open."

"Listen Nelson, grab hold of my arm. NO... my arm! Okay, you feel where my finger is pointing?"

Nelson felt.

"Nice nails."

"Stare over there," ordered Tina.

"But..."

"Stare over there Nelson... and concentrate."

They both stared intensely, which is very difficult into pitch black. There followed a long, pregnant pause, long enough for triplets. No sight or sound, only the occasional catch of Tina's perfume.

"Concentrate Nelson."

"I am."

Nothing.

"Concentrate!"

Then a hiss.

Then a brilliant, thin shaft of light, as if a million-

Watt fluorescent tube had been lain across the floor. The width of the tube expanded. A door was evidently opening inwards to a brilliantly lit room. A pure, white glow was now burning their eyes. The room behind appeared first as a hazy, white apparition - images beginning to coalesce from within. Light poured onto their faces and into the black tunnel.

The room was ultra-clean, painfully white and intensely lit. And standing in the exact mathematical centre of the floor was a bright white cistern and a bright, white bowl.

"Oh God," yelled Tina.

"Another toilet!" spat Nelson. "These Knowalls should cut down on their fibre."

"Turn around."

"What?"

"Turn around and stare at the other wall," said Tina.

"It'll just be a bidet."

"Do it," ordered Tina, more determined than ever.

They focused on the opposite wall, now well illuminated from the toilet. Soon another shaft of light appeared, this time feeling less intense. The opening door did not reveal a bidet, but a hallway. It stretched far ahead of them and leading off at regular intervals were friendlier wooden doors of more traditional appeal. Each one thickly lacquered and brandishing a shiny metallic plaque bolted to its middle.

The word *MUSEUM* 3 was embossed into the floor before them.

They looked at each other.

"Come on," said Nelson and they both ran in. There was hiss as their entrance closed behind.

They ran down the hallway, but Nelson soon slowed to a walk as he took in the curious titles written on each door.

"What?" questioned Tina. "Why so slow?"

"Look."

This was a very strange museum indeed. The titles on the door plaques so far read:

NEURAL FIBRE OPTICS
VIRTUAL REALITY IMPLANTS
FOUNDATIONS OF INTERPLANETARY TRAVEL
LIFE & DEATH BY SOCIAL MEDIA
BIOTECHNOLOGY & TISSUE ENGINEERING

"What is this place?" Tina asked. Although she did not understand the implications of the weird titles, she could sense a disturbing unearthliness about the whole place.

"Harrods," answered Nelson.

"What?"

"Harrods. This must be part of Harrods. They say that you can't see it all in one day so this must be the part you can't see."

"Have you gone mad?"

"Yes."

"Now what?"

Nelson shrugged his shoulders. He contemplated his last twenty-four hours.

"Freaksville. Or Disneyworld. Pinch me."

"Sorry?"

"Pinch me, hard. Just there."

Tina pinched him hard.

"Ow!" shrieked Nelson. "Now let me pinch you."

"No."

"Please."

"No!"

"I'm awake, so it must be your dream."

"It's nobody's dream," said the voice from nowhere.

"Do you work for British Rail!" shouted Nelson to the ceiling. Why don't you try *The train now standing at platform two is the delayed 19:27 for the Moon and will be departing approximately forty years late.*"

Silence.

"In here," Nelson shouted to Tina and nobly tried to pull her through one of the doors.

"Ow!" he shrieked as his shoulder blade slammed into the sturdy door and buckled into his vertebrae.

"Damn you. Try that one."

A door incomprehensibly marked *CLOUD COMPUTING* was unlocked, so they rushed through.

"Ah, do come in. Good to see you again so soon," said the same shaven headed old man dressed in his deep red gown, standing in the middle of the room.

CHAPTER 22

"This is it," said Nelson.

"What is?" asked the old man, gently scratching the left side of his white beard stubble.

"The proverbial it," said Nelson.

"Is it! Do show me."

This time Nelson fully studied this ancient, venerable nobleman stood proudly before them. The hardened lines sunk into his ebony skin and around the hazel eyes framed a faint smile. In the white light of this room his robe of intense vermillion shimmered and enhanced the gold braid that traversed it with intricately laced clouds. He noticed tiny letters stitched into his left shoulder that appeared to layout $D E X$, separated from the number 2 and letter O.

"How did you know we would run into this room?" Nelson challenged.

"Simple prediction analytics," came the reply. "And also, we left this door open."

"You're going to *erase* us," said Tina.

"Well, you have been already my dear."

"Explain it then," said Nelson, "this is Heaven?"

The faint smile transformed into a broad grin.

"Oh no, dear me no."

"Hell?"

"I'd like to quip that you are getting warmer, but no."

"Okay, it said Cloud Computing on the door. Mainframes made of mist? Machines perched in the sky?"

"No Nelson, this is none of those. I asked you before, do you like change? Can you cope with real change – or more specifically, with revolution? Well, if you can, then this… is simply a small part of a whole."

"And we're the toads in it!" scoffed Nelson and

was about to raise two inappropriate fingers when Tina interrupted.

"We panicked. *Erase* suggests removal from the human race?"

The Knowall turned to Tina as she continued.

"That's what your computer said back in the huge chamber."

"It does my dear, it does. But not in the sense that you have obviously interpreted it."

There was a brief pause as they processed this answer and the situation. Nelson spoke first.

"Are you aliens?"

"Ha, ha. No, not at all. But then we're not exactly members of the..." he stopped himself abruptly. "Everything will become clear."

"I am *so fed up* of hearing that," bawled Nelson, "So far it's as clear as a mud pie in a black bin liner. We'd like it clear please. Now."

"As I said, everything..."

"*Now!*"

"Nelson, there is due process here. Mountains have been moved, meetings convened and adjourned. All as a result of your recent conduct."

Nelson stood his ground.

"And we..." he held out his hands towards Tina, "have been *kidnapped.*"

The old man considered his options, eventually resting his eyes on Tina.

"As you insist."

He gently touched a silver disk on the wall. In response another impossibly flat, considerably larger screen, descended from a ceiling recess. It flickered to display a map of the world. On it lay a pulsing red fleck at the heart of Great Britain, tagged to declare *YOU ARE HERE.*

"I told you!" exclaimed Tina.

"I'm sorry?" queried the Knowall.

"It doesn't matter."

Other red spots appeared on the map, but none pulsed. They illuminated Iceland, Puerto Rico, Madagascar, Florida, Sicily, Macau and Tasmania.

"As you can see," began the Knowall, "we are all part of a whole. At all these points we have underground installations like the one you are in. Points where you would least expect to find us. Not that anyone knows that we are here anyway, but it remains very reassuring. We prefer small countries, especially islands. We have a few higher profile channels, parts of NASA you've mentioned, but we'll come to that in a moment."

"Is this going to be a long explanation?" asked Nelson.

"It may be."

"Can we have a seat?"

"Why of course, please relax," said the Knowall indicating a few office chairs beneath the assorted desks and workstations. They organized themselves. Nelson slouched, Tina crossed her legs.

"Now as you know, we are the Knowalls. Perhaps a curious, some could say unfortunate, name. But one I believe to be quite apt. Are you sitting comfortably?"

"Yes."

"Then I'll begin."

The Knowall perched on the edge of a desk.

"We're in the UK, aren't we?" he began, more confirming the fact for his own needs, before continuing, "Yes. So, do you recall your O-level history lessons? The Luddites? We… are in this room, in this very situation, as a direct outcome of the Luddites."

"The who?" asked Nelson.

"No, The Who are a pop group," grinned the old man. "I'm talking about the Luddites from the early 19th century. They were a small group of English labourers in the textile industry - with a lot of public support. And they certainly did not like change."

"Hang on," interrupted Nelson, "what have textile mills got to do with this Cloud Computing thing?"

"Indirectly quite a lot. The Luddites violently opposed the introduction of new machinery into these Isles at the very beginning of the Industrial Revolution. Great Britain was then leading the world in innovation. The Industrial Revolution was born on this island. So, what did the Luddites do? Like any God fearing, law abiding citizens, they revolted. They feared the changes, and the new equipment. They thought it would take away their jobs, their livelihood and their dignity. They rioted and they wrecked it. They were arrested of course, but they underlined the public discontent at the time to the introduction of anything new. Are you with us Nelson?" digressed the Knowall.

Nelson had turned to stare at Tina. She was focused on the Knowall, but for him the words had no coherence.

"Sorry, the Luddites? I vaguely remember my history lessons, but…"

"Nelson, nearly 200 years ago the Luddites were skilled workers who despised the introduction of machinery and destroyed it, fearing for their skillsets and their jobs. Their leaders were arrested, and textile production continued whilst the machinery was repaired. But…"

The Knowall paused as he observed Nelson's concentration wander again to his surroundings and back to Tina.

"Sorry!"

"But, restoring the machinery took a little while and in this intermission the inventors had come up with bigger and better versions, ready to take their place on the factory floor. So far so good?"

"I think so," said Nelson.

"Yes, absolutely," stated Tina.

"So, the inventors of the updated machines agreed

it may be better to wait until the workers became comfortable with the original machines - before they introduced their new versions. And so the pattern began."

"What pattern?" ventured Nelson.

"So, these new releases were stalled. Nevertheless, inventors by their nature, do not sit around idle. They pursued reinvention and refinement. And by the time they trusted the workers ready to accept their second creations, each were already into their fourth or fifth generation machinery."

"Oh dear," anticipated Tina.

"Very well put. *Upgrades* my dear fellows. *Upgrades*. We are talking persistent, unstoppable progress.

Most individuals naturally resist change. They still do, and with industrial machinery this becomes very problematic. But then, enter the revolutionary concept of electricity and you've really got yourself a whole raft of troubles. You see the invention of electricity and its application came as a natural consequence of demand, and the rapid evolution of industrial machinery. Humanity's ability to power these new machines electrically actually emerged just a few years after the Luddite riots."

He paused, as if for dramatic effect. At that instant Nelson's head was down as he idly scratched the back of his own neck, He froze mid scratch. Just his eyebrows arched upwards to meet the Knowall's querying gaze. Nelson had nothing to offer and his eyes rolled over towards Tina, who was staring intently ahead. Awkwardly his dry mouth began to open slowly.

"An even *bigger* change?" burst in Tina.

"Very perceptive my dear."

Nelson's scratch changed to a gentle stroke and on to a massage of his neck muscles. He was suddenly out of kilter and was flooded with recollections of his imaginary numbers' bewilderment in O-level Mathematics, whilst his fellow pupils nodded sagely. This room was so white, its lines so clean, and its screens so ridiculously thin. The left lace on his Adidas trainer was loosening. Tina's ankles were crossed and the leather on her court shoes shone brightly. He knew so few perfumes, but he was sure hers was White Linen by Estee Lauder.

"Yes!" snapped the Knowall. "Electricity! An enormous change. And by now our highly sensitive textile workers were at least four generations of machine behind their inventors... so how could they possibly cope with a limitless, invisible power source? They had been comfortable with breaking their backs for aeons, and being paid for it."

Nelson remembered his schoolboy reaction to the idea of an imaginary number. He shrugged.

"They couldn't cope," said Tina.

"No way José, I believe is the phrase," confirmed the Knowall. "So, the introduction of electricity was also postponed, in the end by about 20 years! If you are still with me, I promise we have nearly finished.

The obvious consequence? Technology crept ahead of the human race - and an elite group was forming, ultimately deciding what, how and when to introduce it. This elite anticipated a future emerging that was in advance of current society. They could also see that this future demanded to remain covert, until the human race was ready for it.

"A secret future?" said Tina.

"Yes, *our* secret future," confirmed the Knowall.

"And it's still going today?"

"It was always designed to be short-lived. It was against their principles to stop progress so they proposed a temporary measure - they would form a secret society to guard the future... and take it *underground*. Which is literally what they did."

"Under Yorkshire?" offered Nelson finally.

"Yes, to start with. At that time Great Britain was leading the way and this very site between the mills of Sheffield and Manchester was chosen as their first. From here they released intermittent innovations, and the Industrial Revolution took off. Albeit much later and slower than it should have. Catching flies Nelson?"

Nelson shut his mouth.

"So, these Luddites… weren't they just a moment in time?" challenged Tina.

"In their way yes, unique. In the Victorian era we were accelerating… photography, rubber, oil, typewriters, electric lighting, we pushed such a variety out.   But humanity always has two hostile factors lurking. War and greed. We started planning our first forays into space in 1917. What were you doing then – one guess?"

"World War I," surmised Nelson.

"Correct. We'd given you engines, petrol and flight and you concentrated on turning them into tanks and fighter planes. Then by the end of 1920's we're finally ready to go to the Moon. And you… have turned rampant capitalism on its head and immersed yourselves in The Great Depression.   So we went to the Moon anyway, without telling anyone."

"But…" started Nelson, "how could you do that without the rest of the world knowing?"

"Another good question. These giant airplane and spaceship launches were very difficult to conceal in those days, but on seeing such a contraption by accident the local populace would report it as a meteor, cloud formation, or even schools of flying fish. Aren't people quaint? And then, wonderfully unexpectedly, the phrase 'Flying Saucers' hit your press. From that moment, we had it made.   If any of our experimental airplanes or interplanetary craft were spotted, they were reported as *unidentified flying objects*, and only a small collection of cranks cared to investigate. Easy.

"UFOs!" said Tina suddenly.

"It's unbelievable," said Nelson.

"That was all we had to do. The rest took care of itself."

The Knowall paused, looked to the ceiling, and took a deep exhale.

"And there you have it." he said, resting his eyes back on the two of them.

Nelson became aware a deep frown had spread over his brow. He met the Knowall's gaze.

"So, a covert underworld... is controlling our secret future?"

"Effectively, yes."

"One question."

"Please."

"What is *Cloud Computing*?"

"I have no idea," said the Knowall. "Maybe you can talk about it later with Bez'0S. Please follow me."

The Knowall led them out of the room and into the corridor. They walked passed the many lacquered doors, and away from the large chamber they had fled. He steered them through another series of corridors. Nelson and Tina walked flanking him either side.

Tina stole a surreptitious look at the figure in his dark red robes. Though he was clearly aging, there seemed something even older and deeper within him, as if a burden weighed heavy.

As they walked in silence Nelson eventually spoke.

"So, what about my NASA letter?"

"Well, indeed there was a Doctor Grimaldi, he was a Knowall."

"So he did exist?"

"Yes. You see, we've always had a handful of our troupe on the *surface*. They are our *progressive missionaries*, tasked with moving humanity's future forward as rapidly as possible. We call them Progressionaries.

We made an exception with Grimaldi and allowed him to stay on the *surface* and be a Non-Executive Progressionary, provided he told no one. Not even his new wife. In retrospect it was our big mistake.

"Why is that?" asked Nelson.

They had reached a T-junction in the corridors. All the floors seemed slightly rubberized, and their steps made little sound. Neatly etched into the wall before them was a large triangle pointing to the left labelled *Laboratory Mezzanine, Keppler Wing, Lifts*. Another tiled tunnel this time in light blue led a sweeping curve into the distance. A similar triangle pointed right to *Reception, Directorate, Cafeteria*. The Knowall walked this way and continued talking. Nelson perked up at the thought of food.

"In 1968, Grimaldi's wife left him. She packed up and walked out one night, never to return. Her note said she knew he was up to something. He was distraught. In his grief he lost all good sense and blamed us for the dual life he was living. He enlisted a small band of like-minded Knowalls and decided to take matters into his own hands, declaring it helped his heartache.

He forged a series of official letters and scattered them across various sites in the hope intellectuals may discover them. He put NASA's name on them, it being one of our main channels - and the place where you will find the biggest group of Knowalls above ground."

"Damn right," muttered Nelson.

"Hmm. And you, Nelson, found what we believe is the last remaining letter, which was slipped into that encyclopaedia nearly fifteen years earlier - but don't tell the publishers."

Nelson and Tina had been stunned. Their eyes glazed and peered to the middle distance as they walked, absent in their own thoughts. The Knowall granted a few moments of silence, allowing his monologue to sink in.

"So… hopefully you can how a Moon landing was possible in 1929. However, Hans Logforn was the first there. His historic words were:

A new world, a new opportunity, a new... Sss. Pop. Thud.

He hadn't sealed his space suit correctly. And at the time President Hoover was completely unaware of it. He wasn't one of ours. A little later we sent a two man mission, just to prove we could do it successfully. It is a fairly boring piece of rock. And finally, humanity caught up in 1969."

Bored with the endless corridor walking Tina stopped abruptly. A few steps in front of her Nelson and the Knowall also pulled up.

"So, do you have a plan to move things forward?" she ventured.

The old man turned his gaze to fix on her and grinned.

"A very perceptive question my dear," he said, stepping a few paces back to be next to her.

"Thank you," she blushed.

"We've been constantly trying, and believed everything was rolling like clockwork during the late 60's and on through those crazy 70's. We released a huge volume to you then. Microchips were everywhere, doing everything, getting smaller all the time. You couldn't get enough, and we put a couple of key tech guys on the *surface* as Progressionaries, to try to speed things up.

"So, we're catching up?" challenged Tina.

"You were. Now you're all feeling threatened by the robot, computers, artificial intelligence and the notion of increased leisure time. So we asked ourselves, *where do we go from here*? And now, thanks to Grimaldi and his cohorts, you two have arrived with the last letter."

"Helloooo…!" interrupted Nelson, "Er… food?"

He indicated onwards down the corridor.

"I'm sorry Nelson, the cafeteria will have to wait a little while," said the Knowall. He then hesitated, seemingly to consider his next words. He held his hands open and looked mutely at them for a long time.

"Nelson, Tina... it grieves me to say that the saddest thing now, is we are witnessing a once promising human race embarking on a journey, that seems impossible to control. A journey that points towards disaster for every one of us.

You are proliferating nuclear weapons.

You are multiplying warheads to the point where even we can no longer keep track. This leaves just one option open to us, which we are now well on the way to achieving. Please, let's walk on. I'm happy to answer any more questions."

A few seconds silence.

"I need to go again," said Nelson. "Where are the toilets?"

CHAPTER 23

"No, no Tina," assured the Knowall as Nelson zipped and vacated another bleached white cubicle to rejoin their walk, "by being erased we're not exterminating you or undertaking anything detrimental to your health. Say, for example, someone unearthed one of your hidden qualities, and you'd really rather they hadn't…"

"Yes," cut in Nelson, "…like when a friend catches you top-shelfing at the newsagent magazine rack?"

A librarial silence descended, the Knowall and Tina turned in bewilderment.

"Not exactly what I had in mind," declared the Knowall finally, "but the parallels are comparable."

He scratched his white stubble again and continued, "In summary, you'd rather their discovery was kept private given the effort you've expended crafting your image."

"That's right," said Nelson.

"Well, we have a lot to protect here and it's why we have to erase you. You know of our existence and we have to remove you from the human race. Your records will be erased."

Two pairs of eyes widened in dismay.

"It's a delicious and sinister expression, which is probably why we use it. It simply means that you will live here now – outside of humanity. And you can be of great use to us."

"What do we have to say in this matter?" challenged Nelson.

"It's clear you need to evaluate your situation," beamed the Knowall. "We're not planning to incarcerate you or similar dramatic action. We simply want to invest in your future and show how you can help us, and we can help you.

"But it would be imprisonment?" quizzed Tina.

"That suggests you have no choice in the matter, and *choice* hangs on how your preference develops. Also, please bear in mind, if you went back screaming about our activities, no one would believe you - and it would severely damage any credibility you have."

"Well, I won't be held against my will," puffed Nelson.

Their walk opened out into the appearance of a reception space. A burnished stone desk of unnecessary length stretched in front of three frosted glass doors, each wide enough to drive a car through. Another impossibly thin monitor rose from the countertop, and a slender, translucent chair was empty behind it. Globular sofas in dazzling orange were arranged against two of the walls. There was a faint smell of sandalwood. The Knowall motioned Tina and Nelson to sit.

"Our desire is for a voluntarily outcome once you've come to terms with our offer and had chance to get to know us. We're a pleasant little community here, with numerous incentives. We'll setup your own Facebook accounts and connect you to the rest of our world."

He widened his eyes and tilted his head faintly, as if the offer were irresistible. No immediate acceptance was forthcoming, so he pressed on.

"Nelson, you haven't really got much of a life in Kilburn have you? We know you're becoming a little jaded with supplement journalism."

"West Hampstead, please." corrected Nelson. "And what's a face book?"

"Not a face book Nelson. Facebook. This will become clear. We've done our research. You've no close friends, distant relatives in Cornwall, and an uncle in Buenos Aires."

Nelson opened his mouth first to protest - but instead he found himself yelling:

"BUENOS AIRES!"

"An uncle Colin I believe – works on vineyard."

"I thought he was dead," said Nelson.

"Apparently not," said the Knowall.

"A vineyard? And who on Earth would buy wine from Argentina!"

"Very few at present, but obviously his disappearance caused you no great consternation. My point being, why not put yourself to some use and stay with us. We genuinely feel you can help."

"The problem i…"

"A telegram has already been sent your most frequent associate – Duke Billingshurst," interrupted the Knowall. "We drafted the simple message '*Got bored. See you sometime*'. He'll assume you're testing an alternative lifestyle and that you're happy - which you will be. Give it a couple of years and you'll be a distant memory."

Nelson opened his mouth to speak.

"And *me*?" grilled Tina.

"Well, I must admit that you are a bit of an unknown. You're young. I hope you don't have a boyfriend, engagement, or similar?"

"Not currently," said Tina. "Through my own choice" she added. "It's not to say I couldn't have, or a job and income, if I chose to, which I don't – and wouldn't – if I stay here – which I might, if I choose to – which I might also."

Another hush descended. Nelson and the Knowall waited.

"What's the matter with you two?" snarled Tina.

Nelson turned back to the Knowall. "So, how far is the human race still behind?"

"Well, given we're in 1983, we've estimated it would take us to 2025 to fully equalize. So, forty or so years," the Knowall answered.

"That long?" exhaled Nelson.

"At least. We've already been to Uranus and back

just to see if the locals like the name we've given it."

"It's inhabited!" exclaimed Nelson.

"No, it's a joke," sighed the Knowall. "We've developed interplanetary travel to the point where we are ready for our final option."

"What do you mean by that?" asked Tina.

"We'll come to that later. Time is pressing. You'll enjoy it here."

"We may have different perceptions of enjoyment," said Nelson.

"Very true. All perceptions are relative. Enjoyment, sorrow, time, shock and surprise. They are all relative. I'm shocked you've listened calmly without screaming the walls down, but then what surprises me may be different to what surprises you."

His focus drifted and a wistfulness emerged. His hand stroked his smooth head.

"All of us experience shock in varying degrees. Do you know the last thing that goes through a flies mind when it hits a car windscreen?"

"No?"

The Knowall smiled.

"Its bum."

On the orange sofa, Nelson's elbows rested on his knees and his hands cupped his chin. Tina absent-mindedly wandered around to the slim reception monitor. It was marked *TOUCH SENSITIVE*.

"You and me both," she muttered.

The Knowall's eyes came back into clarity.

"Funny things – flies," he said finally.

"Hmm?" murmured Nelson.

"Flies."

"Yes…"

"They spend their lives buzzing inanely around some suburban living room and suddenly WHAM! – they're on the front page of a national newspaper. Instant fame you could say."

"Where is all this going?" demanded Nelson and included flies into his theoretical thoughts of relativity.

Could it really be possible for the human race to reject technology to the extent where a select few had to take it upon themselves to deal it out in small doses?

Tina was similarly vexed. She had sunk into the limbo of her own thoughts but was emerging convinced she was beguiled by this venture, setting aside Nelson. Although he was curiously growing on her. Her exciting experiment in north London life had matured into routine, ripened into an *Okay* ranking, and then sudden redundancy. She was restless, longing for a change of scenery and pace, towards a thrill and touch of the alternative. This current situation was beginning to stack up well.

"I think it's about time that you met the others," said the Knowall, "I'm sure there will be a mutual fascination."

He pushed on one of the frosted glass doors. It pivoted near its centre and he beckoned them to follow him in. As Nelson and Tina walked towards it they both noticed a small metal plaque on the door's frame marked:

CENTRAL DIRECTORATE

The door led to another immense room, this time

fully paneled in dark wood, augmented by recessed lighting and an inky blue carpet of outlandish plushness. The tang of finely oiled carpentry hung in the air. The room was occupied by five men and one woman of varying ages, a long, reflective table and a very black dog - a Doberman Pinscher.

The far wall sported a crest carved deep into the woodwork. It depicted an owl perched on a human brain. The owl's intricate eyes scowled intensely at Nelson as he read the words underneath. They said:

WE ARE IMMENSELY CLEVER!

"A little joke by our carpenters," informed the Knowall, "It should have said IN KNOWLEDGE WE TRUST, but you just can't get the tradesmen these days. Do make yourselves comfortable."

Three empty chairs were at the table. The Knowall took one and indicated Nelson and Tina to sit.

Those already seated studied their two new visitors. No emotion was evident on their faces.

Nelson looked at the huge dog. The Doberman Pinscher stared back menacingly, loudly barked five times, growled deeply, and was given a biscuit.

CHAPTER 24

The huge room dwarfed its occupants and chihuahuaed the Doberman Pinscher.

Three of its occupants donned lustrous white robes, each with a thin rainbow braid stitched from sternum to sweep over their right shoulders. The other four, including the Knowall who had accompanied Nelson and Tina, sported the same deep vermillion robes with a variety of gold braid styles. The dog remained raven black.

Nelson appraised the scene. It was undeniably a wonderous sight, yet something did not fit. A strawberry.

From the clean lines of the cherrywood walls, down to the curved lines of the mirrored table, everything balanced.

From the sweeping edges of the long table, pulling focus to the circular porcelain salver planted impeccably in its centre, all was harmonised. But slightly off-centre on that salver sat an isolated strawberry.

Nelson's imagination ignited and primed itself for lift off…

TEN…
This was obviously not a strawberry.

NINE…guidance is internal
In his 1980's surface world radios can be made to look like hamburgers, telephones like cartoon mice, so he had learnt not to be fooled.

EIGHT…
His surface world was now forty years behind this underground realm. So, what could it be that sat there so intimidatingly before him?

SEVEN... ignition sequence starts

Extrapolating the trend in miniaturisation by forty years, Nelson assembled sensational hypotheses.

SIX...

It was a rechargeable strawberry comprising a video camera with satellite dish built into the stalk. It could beam discrete images of each occupant anywhere in the world, on command of the Chairman's voice.

FIVE...
Brilliant.

FOUR...

Or the stalk contained a microscopic laser, and the relevant optical instruments, to reproduce holographic images of a strawberry... and it was not really there at all.

THREE...
Absolute genius.

TWO... all engines running

Maybe, truly maybe, it was banana that had been injected with the appropriately encoded electro-chemicals empowering it to assume the shape and flavour of a strawberry, or any other fruit, at the whim of its consumer.

ONE... LIFT OFF! we have lift off

Nelson's gaze was caught by a white-robed Knowall. In an instant his fantastical speculation was answered.

"Would you like a strawberry?" the Knowall asked, "I'm afraid there's only one left."

WHOOPS... forgot the clutch!

"No?" followed up the Knowall, "Final answer?" and without waiting for a further reply he grabbed the fresh strawberry and popped it into his mouth. He then pitched the stalk to the Doberman.

The dog snapped, swallowed and then growled. He was tiring of endless strawberry stalks and biscuits.

A short silence ensued.

With his curiosity about the strawberry satisfied, Nelson calmed down and considered Tina. He admired her growing composure and her form. The fringe and brunette hair framed an exquisite face and neck, and her raincoat remained tightly belted. She was unaware of his scrutiny, being fully absorbed by the situation.

A new Knowall stood up sharply.

"The pair of them will do nicely," he said.

Nelson snapped back into his seat, quickly realising he was off track.

"Yes, just fine. Welcome… to our underworld."

He was perhaps by far the tallest of their hosts. His deep red robe sported the most elaborate double braid, featuring a procession of gold swans embroidered amongst delicate water ripples. A shock of white hair topped broad shoulders that suggested a strong physique beneath.

"I feel a few introductions are in order," he continued. "Nelson Staff and Tina Reagan…"

"Yes?" said Nelson and Tina in unison.

"Now… which is which?"

Nelson nearly fell of his chair.

"I'm sorry?" he managed.

"Which of you is Nelson and which is Tina? My apologies but it is the first time we've met."

Tina and Nelson stared at each other with the same horror. Picking up on this the Knowall thumbed his swan braid, adding:

"Oh, I do beg your pardon. Sorry, we dispensed

with gender defining names during a management restructure in the early 70's. Though some of us have a recollection of the old formats, it's a challenge recalling which sex they relate to. Let me see - would Nelson be masculine?"

"Marginally," offered Tina.

"Oh, I'm very sorry..." started the Knowall.

"Yes," intervened Nelson, "you are correct. I am Nelson and this is Tina."

"Oh good," said the Knowall, "To make you feel at home we've undertaken to recall our old names. Or, where that hasn't been possible, the nearest guess. Hopefully, it will be more endearing than the likes of Dex'2O," he indicated his colleague that had accompanied Nelson and Tina thus far.

"Or mine he continued, which is Cha'3E."

Lightly touching the swan braid again he continued

"So, instead of Cha'3E, my new name is Charles Arthur Clarke. Or, to promote yet more familiarity, you can call me Charlie."

He then called out the three dressed in white opposite him.

"These are now Mikhail Gee..." a stout middle-aged figure nodded faintly back at them. A striking red birthmark showed on his head through receding hair.

"Then my dearest colleague Emm'8K, now Emma Kay... or back to just Emm, if you prefer?"

The female's stunning light blue eyes were amicable. Her blond hair curled towards her shoulders and fell over the collar of her white robe. She held up a hand to wave. Charlie continued around the room.

"And a couple of our younger members here, Fry'1S, who we have forenamed as Stephen, he prefers the traditional spelling. There are big plans for him."

An apprehensive young man smiled back at them. A fop of dark hair swept down to his left brow and stretched across to the right. He held an unlit pipe in his hand and touched it to his mouth.

"Pleased to meet you," smiled Nelson.

"Good day."

"And by far our youngest member at the table, Bez'0S. We're still working things out, but he may have a huge future, might you Jeff? In our Museum, it was his room that you ran into."

A fresh-faced young man, no older than his late teens, with centre-parted hair and strong eyebrows looked intently into Nelson and Tina's eyes. He spoke efficiently.

"If we stay focused, we can achieve all our goals." He then smiled too broadly and followed this statement with an awkward burst of laughter.

"Thank you. Wise words Jeff, and I know we will be relying on you soon," applauded Charlie, and turned to his remaining colleagues.

"Then we have your new friend, Dex'2O... now Dexter Oh."

Dexter blinked and nodded warmly back.

"Thank you for the tour," said Tina.

"Next to Dexter is our very own Doctor Xing, the principal brains at this table."

Xing nodded at them efficiently and impassively.

Cha'3E, now Charlie, turned to the concluding male sitter, his voice raising appreciably.

"And, of course..." he paused, clearly trying to recall the replacement name for his final colleague. He held out is hand towards the man who was markedly the oldest member of their group, hunched at the table, translucent skin accentuating liver spots across his cheeks, bare head and hands.

A pause hung in the air.

"Gloria!" wheezed the grey face atop the frail body.

"Ah yes, Gloria."

At this last name, Charlie raised his eyebrows slightly in disbelief.

"And there you have it."

Nelson felt the urge to say something but stopped himself.

The dog barked.

"Sorry, of course! Our four-legged friend here is called Bulldog," added Charlie, "previously Zen'K9."

"But it's a Doberman Pinscher," challenged Tina.

"Yes, we are aware of the fact, but yelling 'Sit Doberman Pinscher' would become tedious."

'So, what's wrong with a new name like Rex?" queried Tina.

Gloria wheezed and laughed, coughed, and then laughed and wheezed.

"Rex!" he gasped, "What a ludicrous name."

"Er…" started Tina.

"Don't," interrupted Nelson, "it's not worth it."

He smiled sympathetically at each of the Knowalls.

Everyone ensured their chair was square with the table and placed their hands on its surface.

"So, what happens next?" Nelson asked finally.

"Quite a lot actually," said Charlie. Dexter has filled you in on exactly who we are, how we come to be here and to some extent why you are here."

"Yes, we're quite *filled in*."

"Happy about everything so far?"

"I could say ecstatic, but…"

"A lot to take in such a short space of time."

"It's sinking in," said Tina.

"Good. Excellent. And late tonight we are all going to Puerto Rico."

"Puerto Rico!" exclaimed Nelson.

"Yes. A charming little island."

"Puerto Rico!"

"Let me explain a little," began Charlie reseating himself. "We are the Central Directorate for the Knowalls, resulting in a large degree of duty and accountability. The challenge of controlled technological distribution to a bunch of primiti… to humanity, is proving forever more burdensome. Right now, we still have our Progressionaries amongst you trying to accelerate its adoption. But we've learnt to be delicate and careful. Two of a new team on the *surface* are making steady progress – Gat'6B and Job'6S. Steady, determined progress. What new names did we give them?" he asked his peers.

"Bill and Steve," rasped Gloria.

"Ah yes, our double-act, Bill and Steve. Unimaginative names, but they will do. We asked them take their time, play their characters well, and build up a momentum."

He paused, as if compiling a mental list.

"There's a lot to get through: personal computers, mobile phones, tablets, phablets, private clouds, wearables, and then onto music, media the digital revolution, Call of Duty, cures for malaria… oh the list is endless. And if young Jeff here plays his cards right it will go on and on."

"But we've already got tablets?" queried Nelson. "I take vitamin C every morning. Will it make me live longer?"

The Knowall smiled. After a few seconds he continued.

"Our people must be so careful up there. We all still grieve over what happened with one of our finest assets, Jay'4K. Nobody… nobody, saw that coming. Killed for decreeing a Moon landing before the end of the 60's – it turned out to be a bad move."

Charlie's eyes misted, the first demonstrable

show of emotion.

Nelson and Tina stared at each other in disbelief.

"We were told it was a lone gunman, or the Cubans. Or even the Mafia."

"Of course you were!" snapped Charlie. "Sometimes putting a cover in place is more challenging than implementing the original plan."

He rubbed a thumb knuckle below an eye and recovered his composure.

"So, as part of our scheming we have made a few mistakes, but one overshadows all of these. One vast miscalculation. A cock-up. We trusted you – and it has gone spectacularly wrong."

"What have we done?" probed Tina.

"Many years ago, our scenario analysis predicted a fossil energy shortage if you continued to consume these fuels at such a carefree rate. If you ran the world dry of oil, we forecast all hell breaking loose. So, it appeared that we had only one option."

"Start a miner's strike?" offered Nelson.

"No, Nelson, the years of major strikes are about to be gone forever, believe me. I'm talking about atomic energy. We chose to invest you with the immense power of the atom."

He paused and stared blankly into the middle distance before continuing.

"The idea was tentatively released. And what do you do? Before we even see a nuclear motor, power plant or any controlled experimentation... you've exploded dozens of nuclear bombs and irradiated the atmosphere. Big mistake for you, bad news for us.

And... what can we do now? We're approaching 1984 and it's impossible to ask for the idea back. You are proliferating country by country, America versus the Soviets, East versus West. And as if that weren't enough, our scenario analysis predicts religious fundamentalism and global terrorism on the horizon.

That is very, very worrying. It is now out of control. Our angriest membership wants to kick you where it hurts again. Humanity does not seem to appreciate the true consequences of what you are playing with. And we've lost grip."

Nelson and Tina's breathing deepened as their induction took a chilling turn.

"So, we have another... *option*. You see now, we're letting you have it."

"The kick in the cojones?"

"No. The Earth. We're leaving you to it. We have an immense plan that has been many years in gestation, with a major milestone just ahead. We've called it *The Quit*. So, there you have it. I believe that... is a fair summary?" concluded Charlie, glancing at his colleagues.

He stopped speaking and a round of nods came from the Directorate in confirmation of his words.

"*The Quit*?" queried Nelson, "I'm sorry, but I don't quite fully understand. Is that why we are all going to Puerto Rico... to retire?"

"Ha! No, not retirement. It's quite simple..."

"But, Puerto Rico?"

"My apologies Nelson, there will be more time later to delve deeper. Right now, we the Reds are already late, and must leave you. We'll meet again shortly."

Charlie went to leave. The two other red robed Knowalls stood to join him.

"I've been meaning to ask," said Tina, just before they departed.

"Yes my dear?" said Charlie.

"Well, the different coloured robes - four of you in red and three more in white. Is it to do with your status within the Directorate, your function, or seniority?"

"Oh no my dear," smiled Charlie, "we're playing in a football match this afternoon. This is our kit."

"Oh, I see. And the black dog?"

"He's the referee."

PART THREE
THE TWIDDLY BITS BENEATH STARSHIPS

The future is already here.
It's just not evenly distributed.
2003, William Gibson

CHAPTER 25

Stardate 1 (Still)
Interstellar Superluminal Ether

"It's my Ireenium cape, you know," said Slogg as he and Dzkk walked away from the loading bay and along the corridor. Zero lumbered a little way behind.

"Gosh offered it to me first."

Dzkk smiled back.

"He's leaving, isn't he? And he's going by taking *my* Eggkraft."

"It's somewhat generous of you Dzkk. Have you considered what you are going to replace it with?"

"A Spacetime Donut. I'm going to get me one of those, and non-poultry themed. But in the meantime Captain, it looks as if I will have to accompany you and see out your destiny, until it is fulfilled. And time is of the essence."

"Are you sure you need to come all the way with us? Don't you have other parts of the universe to be masterful in?" asked Slogg.

"Nothing that can't wait."

As they made their way through the ship this unlikely pair continued chatting. Dzkk was enthralled in Slogg's encounter with Gwofie and the Digitari. He was most pleased the numerous crates of the universe's strongest Braevitchkan beer had been secured for the Peacefulness and Primacy Offering. And he adored the idea of a pink elephant onboard.

Following a drink and congratulatory toast in

Refreshment Bay Two, Slogg left the old man to his thoughts and reverted once more to the bridge.

A while later the starship briefly popped out of superluminal drive to lay a rather large egg beneath its fuselage, and Gosh Bordomm hurtled due north, disappearing into the inky blackness. This short delay in transit allowed the ship's pursuer to close in further, its flashing blue and red beams pulsating silently.

On the bridge's immense screen, an oblivious Captain Slogg studied a rare image of the planet he was about to visit and enlighten. Taken many annums earlier by a wayward deep space explorer it showed a very rare blue-green planet of twenty nine percent land mass, covered by swirling white cloud. It was quite beautiful, and they would be there in a short while.

CHAPTER 26

3ʳᵈ September
03:20am GMT, International Airspace

The plane from Yorkshire to Puerto Rico finally departed in the early hours of the following morning. The Knowalls referred to it as their *private jet*, though it was clearly a modified Boeing 707. It bore no markings or logos, but carried a distinctive smooth black coating embedded with gossamer wires across the upper half of its fuselage, wings and tail, supported by a matt white lower belly. It performed an incredibly steep take-off from a landing strip ostensibly too small for an aircraft of its size.

Inside, the standard quadruple passenger seats were replaced by large leather recliners dotted round in pairs or fours, occasional tables fixed to the flooring, a bar, more ridiculously thin computer screens, and what looked like a fully equipped kitchen complete with uniformed chef.

"First class?" Nelson enquired, once his constitution had recovered from the sharp climb.

"No. Just *class*," Gloria wheezed.

The plane levelled off as it reached cruising altitude. The Knowalls were resting, reading or snoozing. Gloria's wheezing subsided. For such a frail man he certainly knew how to wheeze with gusto. Tina stared intently out of a cabin window, entranced by the twinkle of lights below from towns and cities.

Emm was deep in conversation with Charlie listening intently to her, occasionally nodding. She then smiled, put a hand on his shoulder and stood up to take her rest in a separate leather seat.

Nelson saw his opportunity. As Charlie studied the papers Emm left behind, Nelson slid into the vacant chair next to him.

"So, can I ask you a couple of questions?" Nelson started straight away.

"Just a couple?" queried Charlie. He smoothed his swan braid down his chest unnecessarily and adjusted his thick red collar so he could relax further into his seat.

"Where's the engine noise for starters?" began Nelson. "It's the same hum here as that truck you had us bundled into."

"Ah of course. Well, have you heard of photo-voltaics?"

"Solar power?"

"Yes. We started playing with selenium over a hundred years ago. Now we just paint solar panels wherever we need them. And they are so efficient, they even work by moonlight."

"*Paint* them?"

Yes Nelson, photovoltaic paint. The top of this plane and its wings are covered in it. So was the roof of your truck. It powers the galvanic engines. Humanity will get it soon enough."

"Pah! There you go again. Okay next question. I can grasp your secret society and I can understand why you had to keep it secret all this time. But what puzzles me now is... because it's been kept so secret..."

"Yes?"

"Well, you've not been able to let anyone know directly about your newest and brightest discoveries..."

"Please get to the point Nelson."

"So, how can you *afford* all of this?"

"Ah I see, you mean pay for it?" queried Charlie

"Yes, the global bunkers, the private 707 jet, the moonshots, the constant investment required to develop new technologies."

"I see."

"So how do you afford it all?"

"Marketing."

"I'm sorry?" blinked Nelson.

"Very clever marketing," repeated Charlie. "Have you heard of the *hype-cycle*? No? Probably not yet. It was a brilliant idea credited to a small think-tank back at the turn of the century."

"I don't get it," admitted Nelson.

"As we evolved, we needed new ways to release technology – and sometimes create whole new industries. The simplest way became a *startup*."

"A what?"

"A startup. A new company controlled by one or two Knowalls. It recruits talented, unsuspecting support staff, and generously seeds our new ideas into the mainstream. The startup creates the buzz, or the *hype*, around what we are releasing – and the *cycle* starts. At the point the excitement reaches fever pitch, or the top of the hype-cycle, one of humanity's traditional firms usually steps in to buy the startup. And we get lots of money to invest again."

"Okay... but what happens to the Knowalls who launch the startups?"

"There is usually a buzz about them for a little while, but it is always short-lived. Sometimes we ask them to do it again, but mostly they leave the *surface* and it's someone else's go."

"So, all this is going on under our noses?"

"I'm afraid so Nelson, and it has been for a long time, sometimes in the least obvious places. In the mid nineteenth century we started artificial baby-milk in Switzerland; in the US denim jeans, then an oil refiner; the world's first commercial airline in 1920's Holland; credit cards in 1950; and on and on."

Nelson tried to let all this soak in. After a moment's thought he asked:

"But what if nobody wants the new idea?"

"Good question. That is where great marketing comes in. And early adopters."

"Early *what*? All these phrases Charlie!"

"Early adopters. Keep up Nelson. The startup's job is to get the product launched. The marketeer's role is to promote it as the most brilliant, basic commodity that suddenly everyone must have. And then they bring in the early adopter comes."

"How?"

"Well, you see young Fry over there, who I introduced earlier..." Charlie indicated along the plane's interior to a young, bookish man poring over a thin glass slab.

"What's he got there?" quizzed Nelson.

"That's a tablet. We'll get onto those later. Anyway, you may not recognize Fry yet, but a lot of people will soon. He's a real polymath and soaks up knowledge - a true Knowall. In a few years he will pop up everywhere - TV, newspapers, films, anything to get his face out. Once he is instantly recognizable, he will become an early adopter of hi tech. He will make our life-changing technology appear friendly and necessary."

"Hmm, okay, all very clever. So that's how you string together making all this money."

"It's not enough though Nelson."

"What, *why*?"

"We now have even bigger plans Nelson, as you'll find out once we get to Puerto Rico. And they need bigger funding."

"So now what?"

"Go *beyond* the startup."

"Beyond?"

"Put some key Progressionaries in place and let them grow the business to its full potential... rather than sell it. I mentioned Bill and Steve earlier. They'll soon own the world's largest software companies. One each.

That'll keep our plans rolling."

Charlie smiled broadly and widened his eyes. He continued.

"You see, the trick is to create an industry and a product set that no one knows they want until now. That's where the biggest opportunities lie. Then you market the pants off it."

"Amazing," said Nelson. He was truly in awe and vainly imagined what a remarkable story this would make for his Sunday supplement employers.

"Thank you, Nelson. I wish I could take credit but none of these were mine. However, thankfully together with Emm over there we're getting near to our own launch dates."

"Your companies Charlie? You are launching startups?"

"Yes Nelson, or more accurately, *repurposing*. Emm and I are about to invigorate two established industries with new and future-proofed product lines."

"Wow! Okay, please tell me… which two?" pressed Nelson.

"Are we invigorating…"

"Yes!"

"Well," said Charlie, "they are…"

"Please."

"Okay… they are, take-away coffee and bottled water."

"*Pah!*"

Nelson could not contain himself. He then instantly felt embarrassed about his outburst.

"I'm very sorry Charlie… I didn't mean to sound so rude. But… well I must admit, I was expecting something a little more sensational and fail-safe."

"Really Nelson?"

"Yes Charlie. Come on. It's 1983… no one is going to buy take-away coffee when we already have instant coffee at home. And *bottled* water… why would I want to go into a shop and buy a container of water, when I have it available fresh out of the tap?"

"That," said Charlie, "is a good question."

"Sorry. Neither of those will take off."

"Thank you, Nelson. I'll take your advice onboard."

"Hopefully someone has better ideas. You know what you should get into…"

"What's that Nelson?"

"Wheel clamps."

"Wheel clamps?"

"Yes, I think that's what they are called. I saw one in Mayfair the other day. Now they are the future. Poor guy thought he'd be okay parking on a double yellow line, and he was just staring at it. He didn't know what to do. You'll make a fortune from them."

"We'll consider it," said Charlie flatly.

"You should," replied Nelson. "Anyway, what will you do with all this new money?"

Charlie looked at Nelson and his face dropped to a severe expression.

"Well, there's an unlikely clue in one of the company brand names."

"A clue. What kind of clue?"

"Starbucks."

"What? You're still not making any sense Charlie."

"*Star… bucks*," the Knowall repeated.

Nelson glanced up to the plane's ceiling, down to the thick white hair of Charlie's head and then stared straight into his deep eyes. He finally shrugged his shoulders and twisted the palms of his hands gently upwards, inviting the Knowall to clarify matters.

"We have to be ready," was all Charlie offered.

"Ready. What for?"

"*…The Quit.*"

"*The Quit…* you mean shutting your companies

down? That shouldn't take long if you think take-away coffee and bottled water are going to succeed!"

Charlie's face did not change as he stared back at Nelson.

"Okay, sorry Charlie, wrong joke. But still…"

Pleased with himself, Nelson strolled along the plane's interior and sat down next to Tina, a wide grin on his face.

"Starbucks eh? These guys don't know everything Tina."

He pressed the recline button on his leather chair. To his surprise it rolled back to a full horizontal.

He watched Tina carefully recline her own seat, avoiding a fully flat position. He settled into the leather, closed his eyes, and let the early morning tiredness start to come into his body as the plane's electric engines hummed softly in the background.

"Wheel clamps," he sighed to himself, confirming the thought with a gentle nod.

CHAPTER 27

Schtop.

As the lift closed its doors and carried Slogg to the bridge, he stretched his pale blue fingers and yawned. He had grabbed a few hours' sleep and dreamt of pink elephants skating on caged feet around a shattered ice rink.

Schtip.

The door opened to a view of Deluxia, her tail held tight to the back of her legs, scribbling frantically on a report tablet. The bridge's screen was unusually blank. Slogg knew instantly that something was wrong. Firstly, Deluxia scribbled rarely, and always in hazardous situations. Secondly the tablet displayed the distinctive violet heading: *Frantic Scribbling Report 101/P: Hazardous Use Only.*

"What's wrong?" Slogg asked.

"Well..." began Deluxia.

"Let me see the report."

"Captain, it won't do you any..."

"Let me see the report."

"But, you see, it's…"

"Give it to me."

Deluxia held up the tablet. Beneath the violet heading it read:

◆**u 000 !!! ☹☹ &% 999 @ noooooo!

"I see," said Slogg, "that bad?"

"I'm afraid so sir."

Slogg turned to his Navigation Officer.

"Well, what's happened this time Walta?"

The points of Walta Woppedd's ears twitched backwards and he lightly touched his groomed temples with his fingertips.

"Er…" he hesitated.

"Come on man, don't sugar coat it."

"Well, we… are being followed Sir."

"*Followed*. By whom?"

"Our sensors picked up an ultraspeed cruiser. They're a few lightminutes behind us and closing."

"A cruiser, out here?" queried Slogg.

"Joyriders," suggested Tarooc.

"Captain!" interrupted Deluxia.

"Yes?"

"There is something strange coming in over the subluminal radio."

"Well?"

"Er, it sounds like…. well, it's difficult to say."

"Put it through."

Deluxia flicked a switched.

Dirr derr. Dirr derr. Dirr derr.
Wup Wup Wup Wup.

"*Police cruiser*!" spat Slogg.

"*Cops*!" hissed Tarooc.

"*Fuzz*," whispered Walta.

"Walta, can I ask exactly why the police are behind us? Were you speeding?"

"Certainly not Captain. We're getting ready to drop from the ether, and only doing one hundred and eighty-seven thousand kilotecs per lightsecond, well inside the limit for this sector."

"Rear view please Deluxia," ordered Slogg.

She turned round to reveal her back, tail and haunches.

"No Deluxia! Rear view of the *ship*, on the screen!"

"Ah, sorry Captain."

The immense screen flicked back to life portraying a blur of flashing blue and red lights approaching the starship. As they came into focus it was clear they were part of a sleek, white, ultraspeed police patrol cruiser.

"Attention!" came a deep rasping voice straight through to the bridge.

"Drop from superluminal ether and pull over," The same voice entered the bridge and went straight through to the base of Slogg's spine. The hairs on the back of his neck stood on end. His bowels twisted. His legs quivered under the sudden increased weight of his body.

"Are you alright Captain?" Deluxia asked as she watched the pale blue skin of Slogg's face drain to white.

"*Attention!*"

"Are you sure Sir," Deluxia asked again. "You look very unwell."

Slogg whispered very faintly.

"Detective Inspector Clamburxer."

"Sorry Sir?"

"Detective Inspector Clamburxer. Oh *hell*. Oh no. Just what is he doing here! Of all the..."

"Pull over!" came the dreaded voice again, "This is the police."

There was no doubt. The man behind that gravelly voice was none other than Milko Clamburxer of the Galactic Police. Slogg recognized the distinctive rasp and drawl instantly. He knew Clamburxer was once one of the most wanted criminals in the universe, and now one of its highest paid law enforcers. Holozine scandals were full of senior police caught crossing the great divide to corruption, fraud, even murder, whilst maintaining a facade as upholders of justice and truth. Clamburxer had made history by reversing this state of affairs. He left incarceration and rose from raw recruit to Detective

Inspector in less than three annums.

As part of his rehabilitation, Clamburxer spent time under the guidance of notorious psychologist Hola Migola. It was here Slogg first met him, and the two spent many months together in Migola's alleged analysis and therapy.

The psychologist's controversial methods encouraged enmity between his patients and there followed an extended period of distrust and dislike between the two men.

"We're dropping out of superluminal ether," reported Walta.

Wup Wup Wup Wup.
Whirrrrrr.

The flashing blue and red lights guided Slogg's starship to a halt, and unease spread across the bridge.

Given the time that had passed, Slogg wondered if Clamburxer would still remember him. He retained both a fear and hatred for the policeman. At the same time, he had to admire his audacity and achievements.

A few weeks after they departed Migola's care, a young Constable Clamburxer pulled Slogg over for parking his planet hopper on a double-yellow asteroid. Fury and resentment quickly mounted and the two tussled, resulting in the discharge of Clamburxer's Occasional Kill Weapon from its holster... into his own thigh. This caused a deep but instantly cauterized wound.

As the constable writhed Slogg made good his escape, grabbing the Constable's Federation holobook[19] as he left. This final act proved to be Slogg's wisest move of his life. Clamburxer was famed for his poor memory

---

[19] Holobook's automatically record police interactions with the Galactic public for instant multidimensional recall on demand. As an added benefit for Slogg, the holobook also contained the contact details of some very friendly policewomen.

following Migola's experimental cranial-shock therapy.

Although the young constable screamed that revenge would be immediate, nothing had arisen from the incident over the annums.

Until now.

The starship was at rest and the police cruiser drew up beside. Slogg experienced a cold chill while Taroooc and Walta shifted uncomfortably in their seats.

Deluxia announced the police had made an official request to dock and Slogg resentfully granted it.

Five minutes later he arrived at a different docking bay with Taroooc, waiting for the pressure to equalise between the two craft. The doors opened with a faint hiss to reveal a diminutive police sergeant accompanied by the unmistakable Milko Clamburxer.

He stood in a reinforced police uniform with extended shoulders. One huge yellow-gold epaulette curved over his left shoulder displaying rugged ammunition cartridges. The right shoulder braced a dazzling show of medals wrapped into a bronze bird-wing form. A heavy gold chain hung from his black tunic collar to a gleaming law enforcement badge pinned on his chest. A black domed helmet dropped a darkened visor over his eyes. Immense green boots reaching to his knees completed the look.

Beneath the visor Clamburxer's face gave no indication of recognition. Slogg was transfixed in immediate relief and pending doom, and said the first thing that can into his head.

"Welcome aboard, Detective Inspector Clamburxer," broadening a fake smile that made his cheeks ache.

"That's *Chief Commissioner* if you don't mind,"

boomed Clamburxer, "and anyway, how do you know my name?"

The shock of Clamburxer's new title very nearly caused Slogg to miss the gravity of his mistake. Chief Commissioner! That meant ever more power. More powerful than Dzkk?

And then *wham*!

What a complete imbecile! Why had he greeted him by name? What ridiculous, unnecessary familiarity. Clamburxer was no fool and he would not let such an obvious mistake pass.

"Er..." scrambled Slogg, "we see a lot of you on holoTV."

"I didn't know Galactic broadcasts reached as far as these sectors?" challenged Clamburxer.

"Er, no," said Slogg, "but the repeats do."

For now, Clamburxer accepted this bizarre response, appearing to have more pressing matters. He stepped aboard and Slogg watched him limp heavily on his right leg - the leg his Zenpo OKW had scorched so long ago.

"We digress. To finish the formal introductions, accompanying me is Sergeant Obloid. And your name Captain?"

"Slobb," said Slogg.

"Captain *Slobb*? A slightly unfortunate name to take command of a starship," quipped the abrasive voice.

"Yes, I suppose it is really," fumbled Slogg, "I'd never really considered it before. Ha!"

He needed to keep the conversation moving.

"And this is my Biophysics Officer..."

"Toool," said Taroooc.

Slogg's orange eyes involuntarily popped. He was totally unprepared for Taroooc's lie, just as Taroooc was for his. They obviously both incurred mis-spent youths to the extent where evasion or elusion had become their default tactic. Clamburxer threatened to bring those memories flooding back.

However, the next question was typical of the Galactic Police.

"Do you have any alcohol on board?"

"Er, yes," admitted Slogg tentatively, concerned as to what the correct answer might be in this particular sector.

"Then let's have a drink," grinned Clamburxer.

Alk (Alkohol and Light-refreshment Katerer) attempted to self-clean its gears, tubes and pumps after dispensing four of the sweetest, sickliest drinks in its repertoire. As it did so Taroooc carried the offerings to Slogg and their two unwelcome visitors.

"Well Captain Slobb," began Clamburxer, "I suppose you may be wondering why we are here."

"I must say the thought crossed my mind," admitted Slogg, who had fretted over nothing else since he first heard the policeman's menacing voice.

"Tell them Sergeant Obloid," came the order.

"Right," began Obloid. Far slighter and shorter than his superior, he wore a similar black uniform but with no reinforcement, two small epaulettes of braiding, grey boots and no visor on his domed helmet. As he pulled out a Federation holobook, Slogg noticed that it was exactly the same type he snatched from a wounded Clamburxer an aeon previously. The sergeant began to list the charges:

"The display of indecent body parts in a public arena. The retailing of these personal appendages without a license. The soliciting of the naval for... Oh *sorry*, that's the wrong filing."

The sergeant fumbled with his holobook, clicking, scrolling, zooming, and a myriad of text, figures and sketches flashed from its small holographic display.

Clamburxer raised his eyes to the ceiling and shook his head. Slogg was grateful for the interlude, but still his teeth remained clamped in a fixed smile that threatened to give cramp to his cheeks.

Meanwhile, Taroooc appeared very ill. His two front-facing eyes widened further in their flat brow and his cheek skin rippled with tiny green-grey lines. The simple reason being the previous set of charges wrongly selected by the sergeant were most familiar. In fact they had been levied annums earlier against a juvenile Taroooc following a late-night drinking spree on Gapyeargonalong Four.

"Well Sergeant Obloid, have you located the relevant charges?" sighed Clamburxer.

"Yes, oh yes. Here we go. Failure to stop at a red dwarf..."

"No, no! Obloid! Desist, I'll do it myself."

He sat back in his chair and took a sip of his drink as if preparing for the kill. Then he leaned forward and hissed:

"Do you realise, Captain Slobb, that you are in a highly restricted sector of the Galaxy. Not only is that against the law, but this is also *my patch*. It makes me very, very angry, and I could throw the book at you."

"What book?" asked Slogg.

"I don't know. *THE* book."

"Oh, that book. Well... *Dzkk*," said Slogg.

"*What*?"

"Dzkk."

"Are you having a stroke?" asked Clamburxer.

"I think I can explain. We are on a mission. One preordained by the all-powerful being named Dzkk. A mission, I might add, of great importance."

"Great importance eh?" rasped Clamburxer, pulling his helmet visor slightly further down and leaning in towards Slogg.

"Yes," said Slogg, attempting to puff his chest

slightly.

"I have a destiny... to initiate a planet into the Galactic Core."

"I see. And which planet might that be?"

Slogg told him.

"Slobb. Dear me. You are either lying or delusional. These sectors have been under my jurisdiction for some time now, and that particular planet was under a great deal of observation. It is not at all ready to join the Galactic Club. Estimates require it to undergo at least another forty annums of development."

"I'm sorry Commissioner..."

"*Chief* Commissioner."

"... but that is exactly what everyone else has been thinking thus far. Yet it would appear we were all wrong. Ask Dzkk."

"Oh, don't worry Captain, I intend to."

Slogg returned to the bridge accompanied by Clamburxer and his sergeant. Taroooc followed and scurried to a corner of displays and buttons, well out of everyone's way. His Delta Nebulese nerves were jangled.

Slogg asked Dzkk to join them on the bridge, which had taken on a funereal tone due to the police presence.

As Slogg went to sit, Clamburxer examined him quizzically. Thankfully, the lift door hissed open and Dzkk appeared.

"Well Captain Slogg, what seems to be the problem?"

Slogg leapt fitfully from his chair.

"Er, that's Slobb," he wheezed, "Slobb! Isn't it, Dick?" He leaned his head slightly to the side and backwards, trying to indicate who was behind him.

"That's Dzkk," said Dzkk, a questioning look washing over his face.

"There you are you see! We've all got problems, haven't we?" Slogg bumbled up to Dzkk to quickly take his arm. He hoped this was sufficient distraction.

"Wait a minute!" yelled Clamburxer, *"I KNOW YOU!"*

Slogg's orange eyes widened remarkably. His pale blue skin taughtened to white, as his mouth opened wordlessly. He span back towards Clamburxer. His tongue turned arid and his forearms numbed through to his fingertips. His total fear of recognition was manifesting. In the last few minutes, Slogg had naively relaxed, believing he was far removed from Clamburxer's memory. But he was now disgorged by the Commissioner's mind's eye. He felt bare, his uniform transparent, and everyone peered through its cloth, though his skin and innards, and straight to his rotten core. A core that abandoned a badly injured policeman to likely death on a deserted asteroid, simply to evade a parking fine.

Slogg glanced around, scarcely able to see through an internal haze of fear. His mouth formed words, but nothing came out because he had nothing to say. No utterance could ease the sickness he felt. He was exposed, and this was the end of the road, the end of his career - maybe the end of his life?

He stumbled forward with no clear direction of movement. Blurred images belayed Walta standing immediately to his right and he twisted sharply to see thoughtful eyes staring back at him. He knew what Walta was thinking. Slogg observed him visibly sickened by serving under such a disgusting Captain. A man with no morals.

Never in his life had Slogg felt so wretched.

"I know you!" yelled Clamburxer once again.

Oh, that voice - that blaring, rasping, menacing

voice. Each syllable a nail in Slogg's anonymous coffin - spat into space with no ceremony - quickly forgotten due to excreta it contained. With tears brimming his eyes, he tried to plead for Walta's understanding, yet still no words came forth. Fear and guilt had now disabled his body. He wanted to scream the walls down and tell of the hideous accident. Surely Walta knew it had been an accident - he never meant to cripple that young policeman. But Walta simply continued to stare at him inquisitively.

"I know you!" came the bellow as the policeman lunged forward.

Slogg could see the end coming, and he knew the afterlife would bring relief. Oh death, where is thy sting?

"I know you! You're Walta Woppedd aren't you… from *Galaxy's Got Talent!*" yelled Clamburxer as he rushed over to grab the Navigation Officer's hand.

The darkness turned to a kaleidoscopic blur.

As Slogg regained consciousness a realization dawned, he was caressing Taroooc's hand.

"Captain, are you alright?" asked the Delta Nebulan.

"Wh… hmm? … don't leave me."

"You passed out Sir. Why did you pass out?"

"Wh…. nnnng…."

"It's okay Captain. Perhaps you are over worked."

Slogg focused beyond Taroooc. Dzkk and Deluxia gaped back down at him, their faces portrayed genuine concern. To his right he became aware of Walta and Clamburxer in deep conversation.

"…but it was so long ago," Walta was saying.

"Yours was the *best* season. I watched every episode."

"Wow! Thanks," blubbed Walta.

"What was the name of your band again?" Clamburxer quizzed hoarsely.

"*A Flock of Beagles.*"

"That was it. Strange name, great music. Loved the hair."

Walta was lost for words and just smiled, lightly caressing his shaped quiffs above each ear.

"*Galaxy's Got Talent*[20]. I miss that show," reminisced Clamburxer, oblivious to the scene behind him.

Slogg turned back to look at Taroooc. He became fully aware he was holding his hand and quickly shook it free. He looked into to Deluxia's caring eyes and managed a weak smile.

"What happened Captain?" she asked.

Slogg stood up and straightened out his tunic. He strolled casually to his large chair and sat carefully.

"I was testing Emergency Procedure 9F."

"Oh," said Taroooc, "and what is that?"

"To deal with sudden incapacitation of your Captain. The protocol dictates immediate action by senior crew members to attempt resuscitation, maintain security and ensure safety of the ship. And... *every last one* of you failed in this duty!"

"But, you only passed out for a few seconds," Taroooc informed him.

"That is totally peripheral".

"And when I rushed over to see if I could provide immediate assistance you grabbed my hand and cried *Mabel, don't let them get me.*"

"I had to appear convincing," lied Slogg. He leaned back in his chair and feigned deep thought. Then abruptly leant forward and slapped the padded armrest.

---

[20] Galaxy's Got Talent searched the known universe for amateur purveyors of entertainment, proffering the thinnest hope of minor celebrity. It ran for 2,762 seasons, only being cancelled when its producers discovered more individuals had appeared on the show than had ever watched it.

"*Right*! Let that be a lesson."

This regained Clamburxer's attention, but Slogg powered on.

"Walta, as principal failure you'll have to work through your lunch break. We're on a critical mission and I have a destiny. So, Chief Commissioner Clamburxer, this is your patch, can you please tell us the way to our planet."

"That's easy," said Clamburxer, "We're nearly there. Straight on for the next fifteen and a half billion kilotecs…"

"And then?"

"Turn left at Jupiter."

CHAPTER 28

3rd September
05:15am AST, Puerto Rico

Tina slapped Nelson on the face.

"Nelson!"

She slapped him again.

"*Wake up*!"

Nelson woke up. He peered around from his partially horizontal position, trying to focus. They were still on the plane to Puerto Rico.

"Keep your *hands* to yourself!"

"What?"

"You know very well."

"But..."

"I think you've been dreaming Nelson. Or should I say, I *hope* you've been dreaming. You whispered, *Let me get it*."

"I wanted to get... the gun in your coat," said Nelson helplessly. "He was the Black Squirrel."

"*Really*?"

"Oh dear..." his voice trailed off. "He was going to kill you. And he didn't like the pilot..."

"Get a grip," said Tina putting her earphones back on.

"I was trying to..." whispered Nelson to himself.

He rubbed his eyes hard and patted his cheeks. The right one still smarted. She was a strong woman.

As he raised his seat, he sensed the plane was in descent and looked out of the window. Expecting to see city lights he saw only the darkness of a forest far below, the tops of dense trees occasionally washed by a distant, harsh light.

He presumed they would land amidst more

seclusion and turned his head towards the dawn sky and wondered on the current time zone. The hour seemed very irrelevant in the present context, so he refrained from asking. The only way he had of telling the time was with the tiny LCD built into his expensive biro, and, typically, this needed yet another biro to adjust it. Another wonderous innovation; one step forward - two steps back.

A stewardess asked everyone to fasten their seatbelts and stop smoking. Nelson noticed Gloria hurrying back to his place, a tang of tobacco odour in his wake. He sat with another heavy wheeze.

"Been for a fag in the loo?" quipped Charlie as the old man gasped for oxygen.

"No, just a chat and a ciggy with the pilots," wheezed Gloria. "From the cockpit there's a wonderful view of the sun coming up over the Arecibo Observatory."

"Good. Looks like it will be nice weather for us," replied Charlie, "And *them*."

CHAPTER 29

Out in deep space a starship made its final computations and manoeuvres to complete a left turn at the planet named locally as Jupiter. Undocked and slowly easing away from this starship was a much smaller craft containing a lonesome Sergeant Obloid. Escaping the massive gravitational pull of Jupiter, the ultraspeed police cruiser accelerated to the nearest interstellar café.

Dzkk retired to the starship's *SPA* bay[21]. He left two distinct emotions steeping the bridge. Relief, from Taroooc, following Obloid's departure, with his juvenile misdemeanours and their 3D reconstruction confined to the Sergeant's holobook. Anxiety, from Slogg, as Clamburxer remained to haunt him for some time to come.

Slogg now stood with Clamburxer in the middle of the bridge, watching as the colossal gas giant swept across their vast screen.

"But surely Chief Commissioner, you no longer need to accompany us for the rest of the journey. It's an insignificant little planet. It doesn't warrant the attention of your standing," pleaded Slogg. "And Dzkk assured you our intentions are entirely honourable."

"That's all very well Captain Slobb, but I remain convinced this planet is not ready to join the Galactic Club - and will not be for some time. Its inhabitants are still heathens. And… something is still bugging me around here that I just can't lay my finger on. I feel as though I'm staring it in the face. Do you ever get that feeling?"

"No, never!"

Slogg turned immediately away and went back to his seat deep in thought. He needed a means to distance

---

[21] Sauna, Plunge Pool and Arousal.

himself from the senior policeman, something to disrupt their close proximity.

"Captain," said Deluxia, "Maintenance Crew have reported successful stowage of our prize pink elephant."

She adjusted her miniature earpiece as further information came in. Slogg remained preoccupied.

"Sir, they finally coaxed it inside cargo bay six alongside the Braevitchkan beer. They believe its familiar aroma helped."

Slogg's mind was frantic. If only he could find a way to distract Clamburxer, incapacitate him, or deposit him somewhere else… until he fulfilled his destiny.

"Sir?"

Or all three!

Slogg tuned in.

"Yes Deluxia." He beamed at her. A miraculous idea had hit him.

"Maintenance have reported…"

"Yes, I heard you. Cargo bay six, alongside the strongest beer in the universe."

Slogg looked back at Clamburxer.

"Er, Chief Commissioner..." he started tentatively.

"Yes?"

"I couldn't help noticing, as we deliberated over our drinks earlier, that you appeared to be quite a connoisseur on the subject."

"I don't remember?"

"Yes. Well, forgive me for being presumptuous, but I'm sure that we can offer you a drink… of the like you may never have tried before."

"Oh, you do, do you," replied a wary Clamburxer.

"Have you ever heard of Braevitchkan beer?"

"Vaguely."

"Ah, excellent. Well, it has a reputation for being one of the finest brews in the universe. In fact, its planet of origin is now inhabited entirely by monks who have devoted their lives to its research, development and brewing."

"Really? Well, I am on duty, but…"

"Oh, fear not. This is a light brew with a delicate fragrance. Not a single jot will it affect your career."

Most of the crew stood silent and dismayed by what they were hearing. They were all fully cognizant that even a sniff of the pure brew procured as their PPO from the Digitari, was enough to dispense a wide grin that lasted for days. However, no one chose to intervene on this peculiar conversation.

"Would you be interested?" Slogg asked.

"Well, when you put it like that…"

"Oh good. We've just taken delivery of a few select crates from an exclusive distribution fleet. Follow me to the cargo bay and we'll crack open a bottle or two."

"Okay! Well, what are we waiting for. That sounds like a good idea to me," said Clamburxer following Slogg to the lift, "Do you have a bottle opener?"

"Good thinking," said Slogg wryly.

"And a crane to pick you up afterwards," muttered Taroooc.

"Sorry?" queried Clamburxer.

"I said you might also need a crate opener."

"Thank, you… Toool!" snapped Slogg, "I'm sure we'll manage."

"Captain," called Walta as the lift door opened.

"Yes?"

"A new planet has just appeared on the scanners."

"Oh good, that'll be it. Put us in orbit Walta, and don't forget cloaking shields. We don't want them detecting our presence too early, do we."

"Yes Sir."

Schtop.

The lift door closed.

CHAPTER 30

The 707 landed on a small, secluded airstrip in the middle of a Puerto Rican forest. As it approached the runway Nelson spotted a stunning and unbelievable sight from his window. They had descended over a colossal concrete dish that appeared embedded into the forest floor. From Nelson's viewpoint the bowl must have been at least one thousand feet in diameter. In the early dawn light he could faintly make out three needle-like structures surrounding the bowl supporting a cable-tethered central mass in mid-air.

Nelson descended the stairway into the warming dawn air. In front of him strode Tina - her heels clicking on the diminutive concrete runway and her raincoat staying tightly fastened.

"Did you see that?" Nelson hissed to her.

"What?"

"That giant stone bowl... as we landed. Who could build such a thing!"

A set of powerful spotlights disturbed the sunrise air, picking out a route towards a shadowed entrance into the forest. Above the treetops and backlit by the indigo and deep red of an early morning sky, Nelson could now discern the three towers reaching skyward that he had witnessed on landing. They supported an immense triangular shaped structure via tensioned steel cables. He slowed his pace to take in this incredible view.

"Welcome to Arecibo," said Charlie turning to his left.

"What is that!" asked Nelson, awestruck.

"Let's get inside and we'll show you."

The group approached the darkly shaded opening surrounded by the dense foliage. A mechanical sound triggered strange motion as the nearest trees began to move unnervingly. They arranged themselves to form a perfect circle that encased their occupants.

From this, the ground that comprised the whole inner circle, minus the trees, began to sink slowly into the earth and rock below.

"Oh my!" exclaimed Nelson standing rigid, unable to move as he watched the needle towers, night sky and spotlights disappear, to be replaced by a dark rock face as they dropped deeper and deeper.

Nelson's sudden shock was replaced by fascination at the level of technical expertise their hosts possessed. They burst into sudden white light and another colossal and brilliantly lit cavern. While his senses reeled Nelson became aware their descending platform was something akin to a huge stalagmite.

They came to a slow halt in a state of limbo, balanced at the midpoint of a wall that formed the giant cave.

Then a shimmering glass walkway, lit by an invisible purple light, extended gently out to meet their own standing rock. Where these two unlikely objects met Charlie carefully strode forward. Each of his Knowall colleagues also took a step forward to their own respective edge of the platform.

"A purple glass walkway!" muttered Nelson to himself.

As Charlie stepped onto the walkway, their huge floating rock began to slowly rotate, offering the glass ramp to the next Knowall in turn. One by one they shuffled, and this crystal exit was offered finally to Tina and Nelson. Nelson pulled alongside Gloria while the stalagmite began to make its ascent to fill the open void it had created to the edge of the cavern roof.

"Tell me," said Nelson to Gloria, "have your lot never heard of a good old door, and maybe a flight of stairs?"

"Of course," coughed Gloria, "here they are."

Before them was a door.
Behind it was a flight of stairs.
The group used them both.

Not a great deal happened in the next five minutes.

"Okay, I take your point, that was boring," said Nelson, four hundred and thirty-one steps and two doors later.

They continued down steps made of steel, some of wood, and some cut from the rock face. Down spiral stairs, down straight stairs, some well-made, some dangerous. But never upwards.

"This is boring," stated Nelson, "Where are we going?"

"Downstairs," replied Gloria.

"And when we get there will there be a little man with red skin and matching cape waiting for us complete with horns and a trident?"

"Probably."

"Nelson, just keep walking," pleaded Tina.

The little man waiting for them at the bottom had grey-white skin and matching lab coat with glasses and a clipboard.

"...seven... eight... nine. Oh good, I think we can start," said labman as he ticked Nelson off on his clipboard. He closed the door to the stairs from which they arrived.

Nelson followed Gloria, who was following Tina and the rest of the Knowalls. They emerged into what felt like open air.

On looking up Nelson realized they were now at the base level of a truly immense cavern into which they started their descent via its ceiling.

"This is... enormous," gasped Nelson, "Ginormous!"

"Infinite," sighed Tina.

"Not quite, but it soon will be," said Charlie.

"Sorry?"

"It'll be more exciting if I just let you witness it," beamed the Knowall.

The cavern was indeed monumental. Within its brilliantly lit interior, white coated men and women worked feverishly at a variety of thin screens and keyboards, or tapped slim glass slabs in their palms whilst checking each other's readout. The tension appeared palpable in anticipation of a great event. But it was the ceiling of the cavern that struck Nelson the most. It was perfectly concave resembling a monumental, inverted dish. A realization struck him.

"Is that the underside of that giant concrete bowl I saw as we landed?" Nelson asked Charlie.

"A superb deduction Nelson, well done. It is by a huge margin the largest receiver... *and transmitter*... ever built."

Nelson turned his attention to the feverish activity.

"Something is about to happen is it?" he sniffed.

"Yes, you could say *something* is," answered Charlie.

CHAPTER 31

Deep in an obscure cargo bay of a starship belonging to the Galactic Fleet a faint giggling could be heard. To trace the source of this giggling one had to pass three crates of MegaMammoth droppings[22], then over four crates of gas masks and safety goggles[23].

Beyond these obstacles and past the cage containing a huge pink elephant, there slumped a rather well lubricated member of galactic law enforcement. In fact, Chief Commissioner Milko Clamburxer was so well oiled his gears were beginning to slip.

"Dee doo… do you know wh... wh... wha' the funniesh thing of all is?"

"No, what?" queried Slogg.

"I… *hic*… I haven't even ha… had a drink yet!"

"Really?"

This was true. Clamburxer had removed the top from the first bottle of Braevitchkan beer. He pushed up his helmet visor, held the bottle in his hand, and stared at the label. This had been enough. Within ten seconds the brew's fumes had taken effect.

"An… and do you…. yooooo *hic* you know what else?"

"What else?"

"Y… you look awf… *hic, giggle* you look awfully stoooo… stupid in that gas mask!"

"Well, you know me," said Slogg, "anything for a laugh. Let's have a drink."

They sat together on a modest bench by the pink elephant's cage. Slogg took the Braevitchkan beer bottle from Clamburxer's unsteady hand and poured them both

---

[22] Traded as a deodorant by the tribes of Detton Nine.

[23] Readied for the ship's next visit to Detton Nine..

a drink into two small glasses. A dark amber ale poured heftily out crammed with swirling bubbles that slowly formed a creamy yellow head. Clamburxer pushed his visor even further back, carefully focused on his glass for a few seconds and then said:

"Well, down the *hic* hatch," and slung the liquid into his mouth. A few seconds later the hatch was involuntarily opened again, and the liquid was thrown back up.

"Pace yourself my dear Clamburxer. This drink needs respect," said Slogg as he watched the policeman's head wobble, and his eyes roll.

Slogg knew the power of the amber brew. He managed to don a Detton Nine gas mask with perfect timing as Clamburxer opened the first bottle. Slogg leaned slowly back on their bench and surreptitiously emptied his own glass quickly into the elephant's drinking trough - then watched in astonishment as the liquid was immediately sucked up by the beast's trunk. He turned back to his guest.

"You see Chief Commissioner, we must not drink it so fast. The Braevitchkan brew needs tender treatment, reverence and a degree of elegance to allow for maximum appreciation."

"Sod the ten-ton tree-men, reverends and degrees for elephants... pour meeee, me another one!"

Slogg happily obliged and watched Clamburxer sip gently through the yellow froth. Somehow this sample stayed in his stomach. With his visor up, Slogg could see Clamburxer's eyes appear to focus intently in the very far distance, then his head wobbled again. He gripped his free hand to the edge of the bench and turned to Slogg, fixing him with a very strange look – an expression Slogg couldn't quite determine. He quickly poured himself another glass, and as soon as Clamburxer's eyes started to roll again he immediately tipped it into the same trough, and once more it was instantly devoured by the elephant.

As Slogg's safety goggles gently misted up, Clamburxer continued his unsettling gaze.

"Do you... yooooo *hic* know," he leaned forward as he saw Slogg attempt anxiously to clear his vision, "you are the besh... the besh, the best looking woman I have seen for a very long time."

"Really?" squirmed Slogg.

Clamburxer sidled closer to him along their small, shared seat.

The expression on Clamburxer's face finally dawned on Slogg.

It was drunken lust.

"Come here my boo... beauty, and let me whisper *burp, hic* in your ear."

"I do not want burp-hic whispered in my ear thank you," announced Slogg, leaping from the bench to avoid Clamburxer's flailing arms.

"Tease!" yelled Clamburxer.

Keeping a safe distance, Slogg topped up Clamburxer's glass to the brim and poured what was left of the mighty beer into the pink elephant's trough. Clamburxer smiled towards him, maintained his grip on the bench's edge, then refocused on his glass without losing a drop.

Slogg turned to leave and began his trek back past the various crates, replacing the gas mask once he knew he was at a very safe distance.

Schtip.

The cargo bay doors opened with a refreshing hiss and he walked out.

Behind him he heard Clamburxer giggle as the pink elephant collapsed.

Once in the corridor Slogg made his way to the

nearest intercom. He pressed the bridge button and asked Deluxia to put him through to Walta.

"Hello, this is Walta Woppedd. Are you receiving, over?"

"Shut up Walta. Just tell me if we're in orbit of the desired planet."

"Yes Captain, but..."

"That's all I wanted to know. Is Taroooc there?"

"Yes Captain, but…"

"Shut it Walta. Just ask Taroooc to join me in the Teleport bay. Have Maintenance Crew prepare these Braevitchkan beer crates to follow us once we announce our Peacefulness and Primacy Ceremony."

"Captain…"

He flicked the switch off and stomped away to ready himself for greeting the people of his destiny.

He hoped their greetings would not involve ridiculous tribal dances or the revealing of private parts[24]. He would find it very difficult to keep a straight face.

Taroooc was waiting for Slogg as he arrived at the Teleport bay. The Delta Nebulan grinned and asked after Clamburxer.

"Oh... I don't think we'll have to worry about him for quite a few hours, hopefully even days."

"Sir… Walta has advised us to wear our Kolidium thermals again. And the atmospheric correction helmets."

"Really? Not another cold planet! I thought this one presented a modicum of comfort?"

"Just to be safe Sir. He was banging on about something, but I always find him quite difficult to listen

---

[24] Interspecies greeting ceremonies remain a social minefield. Each genus may consider different parts of their bodies to be private. On the moons of Olfact One, indiscreet visitors can be arrested for picking their nose.

to."

They pulled on their suits and attached the helmets. Small green numbers flickered to life within their head-up displays.

"So Clamburxer is still alive then?"

"He's still alive. I just don't think he'll have any control over his actions whilst we fulfil this destiny and get at least a billion kilotecs away. I must say, I'll be glad when this is all over. The novelty is wearing thin. Are you ready to meet the people?"

"Er, yes. But..."

"Good. Right then," and Slogg turned his attention to the Teleport engineer, "could you place us on the land mass with the highest population, and could we preferably arrive on a slightly raised plain to make addressing the thronging millions a little easier."

"You've got it Captain," said the engineer.

"I know I have," replied Slogg.

The Teleport Stream warning light began to flash in the bay, it said:

REMEMBER: CLOSE YOUR EYES.

The swirl of high energy electrons deposited Slogg and Tarooc close together on a small boulder, raising them very marginally above a surrounding barren landscape, completely devoid of people.

"Very funny!" snapped Slogg, "Teleport engineers are so bloody minded. Ask for high population density and they stick you on a stone in the middle of a desert."

He stepped down and surveyed the panorama. The immediate vicinity was covered in orange sand, brown earth and small rocks. The horizon showed similar coloured hills fusing into a red sky illuminated by a weak sun. A chill began to bite through Slogg's insulated clothing and Taroooc was already shivering. Slogg turned to him in desperation.

"It's cold, *again*! And the helmet tells me this air is so thin. But the initial reports told us it was safe to breathe. And… a desert is no place to announce your arrival from outer space. So, what was that idiot doing putting us here?"

"But Sir, that's just what I was trying to tell you as we left," started Taroooc, "Once we were in orbit our scanners were unable to pick up any standard life-form readings. It seems something terrible has already happened here. There appear to be no lifeforms."

"*Armageddon*?" hissed Slogg.

"We think so Sir."

"You mean we're too late!"

"Possibly. Just by a fraction."

"But what about my destiny? Another planet that finally really did it!" Slogg then called skywards. "You maniacs! You blew it up. *Damn you*! Damn you all to…"

"Er, excuse me…" said a small voice.

"Shut up Taroooc!"

"I didn't say anything," said Taroooc.

"Then what…"

"Excuse me," said the voice again, only this time a little more pained.

"Who said that!" Slogg and Taroooc exclaimed together.

"I did. Would you mind stepping off me?"

"What!"

The small rock you are standing on, would you mind moving from it, I'm underneath."

Slogg and Taroooc both took a leap to one side.

"I'm here," squeaked the voice, as a stone that had been beneath Slogg's boot quivered, almost imperceptibly,

Slogg crouched cautiously to gently lift the stone and peer underneath. He was stunned to see a tiny, slug-like creature, slither smoothly out, complete with two sad eyes and mouth set in a pained grin. Surprise enough, but the miniscule mollusc was dressed in a dark-grey overcoat, pin-stripe trousers, spats, and began propping itself up by a gleaming walking cane held in one of its tiny tendrils.

"Good evening gentlemen," began the creature, "allow me to introduce myself. I am Blupin Slingsling, but you can call me Blupe. Welcome to our amusement park. Admission free."

As a starship Captain, Slogg had become accustomed to encountering exotic species. This took it to a new level.

Taroooc glanced casually over Slogg's shoulder, commenting that a walking cane was a more appropriate accessory for top hat and tails, not an overcoat.

"But I need the walking cane," put in the creature's tiny voice, "it's very difficult to walk upright as a gastropod."

"Okay, okay. Just a minute, let's slow things down a little," interrupted Slogg, holding up his hands and spreading wide his blue fingers.

"You're a slug - that talks..."

"I prefer *gastropod*," put in Blupin.

"... and Taroooc seems to know the current sartorial requirements for slugs. Gastropods. And okay, you need to carry a walking cane. But... I don't see what *any* of this has got to do with an amusement park. Hmm?"

"Why sir, look around you. Over there is a rock, with two more rocks just beyond it. In the middle distance is a sandpit, and next to that... three smooth pebbles! Such a maelstrom of fun."

"You're quite easy to please then?"

"Possibly."

"But I don't see..." began Slogg,

Blupin cut in.

"I can see that as a bipedal species you are not

very impressed Sir. Well, if you desire a real treat, may I suggest that you stroll over yonder hill to discover our latest arrival."

"And what might that be?" asked Slogg bluntly.

"Ah, well… a very lavish vessel."

"Vessel?"

"Yes indeed. None other than a *Viking spacecraft*."

"A *what*?"

"A Viking spacecraft, it says so on its plaque. Okay, it may not be very impressive to you walkie talkies, but it is quite a good laugh for us. It sits there digging holes in the same piece of sand at regular intervals. Highly amusing."

"And what is the point of your spacecraft doing that?" Slogg asked.

"Oh, it's not *ours*," Blupin corrected, "Good heavens no. It was sent here by one of those other planet thingies up there - so I'm led to believe."

"Other planets?" pondered Slogg, "And just where are we?"

"The amusement park."

"I know that. But where exactly? What planet?"

"Why, planet Mars of course."

"*MARS*!"

"That's what we call it."

"But we wanted *Earth*!"

"Well look around you old fellow, there's tons of the stuff."

"*Planet Earth*," shouted Slogg, his voice full of disbelief.

"Oh, ha! You mean the duffers who sent down that Viking thing to find life here. What a bunch of cowboys. I mean, what self-respecting group of scientists would send down a box of tricks like that… to look for life on another planet."

"But…" began Slogg.

"*All* it ever does is dig the occasional hole with

that long black arm, and then examine the sand. Boring! And *all* we had to do was get out of its way when it first made the big fuss of landing. From then on it has been easy avoiding the great lump. When it first got here there used to be this almighty whirring noise as it tried to photograph us. We'd here the buzz and just have great fun hiding under the rocks. It's a good job it couldn't hear us giggling. Truly backward. Truly amazing."

Slogg stared incredulously at Taroooc.

"We've got... the *wrong, damn, planet*!" he bellowed.

"What on Mars would you want to visit Earth for?" exclaimed Bluepin Slingsling.

"We have a certain job to do, thank you. So, I am afraid it is time for us to leave."

"Well, I wouldn't waste my time with them if I were you," smiled Blupin. "Do you chaps know the real irony with that Viking lander? No? Well, it has taken millions of photos of our rocks, and *they* are the planet's most intelligent life-forms. Ha!"

At which point the rock, from under which the little slug had crawled spoke:

"Excuse me *dahhling*... would you mind putting me back on top of little Blupin here. We were having a very meaningful exchange."

CHAPTER 32

Under another enormous rock something else was about to happen.

In the cavern beneath Puerto Rico with its concave roof, men and women in white coats became a flurry of action as they dived from touch screen to tablet to 1983-style computer print-out.

"What we are about to attempt has only been achieved once before, and then there was some instability," Charlie informed them.

Nelson felt the urge to look up. Way above him was the concave cavern ceiling, the man-made underside of the immense satellite dish above. As he searched for some clue to the forthcoming extravaganza, he became aware the lighting of their vast underground chamber was dimming.

Far in the distance an engineer announced in an officious tone that full power was now available.

A faint hum vibrated to fill their surroundings, rising gradually in tone. Nelson noticed his hosts were starting to lift their gaze to the cave roof. He nudged Tina to indicate this and both felt compelled to stare at the curved ceiling. The thrum began to rise and fall, deeper and deeper, until it reached into the lungs.

The air filled with anticipation. All eyes glued to the now dark cavern roof.

Charlie spoke as he gazed upward.

"You see, Puerto Rico has been selected to be the most important meeting point in the history of the Earth."

"Meeting point?" grilled Tina.

"Yes. And it was picked for two reasons. Firstly, a natural dip in the rock that forms the Arecibo Observatory and dish… we'll come to that in a minute. And secondly because it is the only place in the world where iron ore, silica and trace elements of boron can be found in the right saturation levels."

"Oh, I see," said Tina, who didn't. "But you just said *meeting point*?" she pressed.

"I suggest that you keep looking up there," said Charlie, pointing to the cave's ceiling.

The deep hum bestowed the impression of a huge force strengthening around them. No one moved in the cavern as an invisible power took control.

The lights dimmed still further, and just the eerie glow from thin screens providing dramatic twisted shadows.

The indented ceiling appeared to undulate, then recede ever further until it disappeared completely. Nelson tried to focus on the dark cement that was there just minutes earlier. Pinpoints of light appeared at random, dotted around the rock.

But there was no rock, or cement.

Suddenly the deep orange and purple of an early morning sunrise shimmered into view.

"Wow!" yelled Nelson, "My God! It's become... invisible."

"Well observed," applauded Charlie.

"That's the sky! At least forty feet of rock - and we can see straight through it!"

"Correct."

As their eyes adjusted to take in the dark morning sky, it became clear the three towers that Nelson spotted earlier were now rising directly above them, appearing as needle shadows reaching to the heavens. The thick steel cables became visible stretching inward from each tower to tightly suspend a peculiar triangular mass. This was centred perfectly above them.

"But where has the rock gone?" asked Tina.

"Oh, it's still there," Charlie assured her, "silica, boron, oxygen in the atmosphere... these are the main constituents of glass!

"Glass."

"Yes. We've temporarily readjusted the rock's molecular structure so that you can see straight through it. And I must say it has worked perfectly this time. Well done everyone."

Nelson goggled in wonderment. If the shimmering purple walkway somehow soured his feeling of bewilderment, then this spectacle certainly revived it. Amongst the towers' shadows he watched a few stubborn stars play out their twinkling as daylight took over.

"As I was saying," began Charlie, "this is the only place in the northern hemisphere that we know of where this is possible. By applying electric and magnetic fields in the right environment and inducing a small amount of high frequency vibration in the iron ore, the molecules are invited to come together, line up and become transparent. At least that is the press release anyway! It's primarily Doctor Xing's idea, and he's been known to perform some strange little dances to make it work."

The slightly built Asian who had flown with them from Yorkshire glanced over with a very broad grin across his face. He nodded in acknowledgment and they all responded with appreciative smiles.

"And…" concluded Charlie, "…it provides a very adequate viewing area for when *they* arrive."

The sunrise began to light the top of the cave, the tips of the towers above them, and finally illuminate the triangular gantry formed of steel girders suspended over their heads.

Nelson was aware of Tina standing next to him and together they contemplated this magnificent view. They stared through invisible rock, past a web-like framework, beyond the Earth's multi-coloured atmosphere and out towards the fading stars. Nelson was genuinely moved and a desire to sigh deeply came over him.

"You know," he exhaled and turned to Tina, "it's at

times like these that I wonder how we all got here."

"Well, Nelson, I'm no scientist, but believe the theory now goes it's all to do with a Big Bang."

"Oh, certainly not," replied Nelson, "my parents were much more sedate."

CHAPTER 33

The universe is very big.

Indeed, it is big enough to get lost in - which many of its inhabitants do.

Slogg wished his Navigation Officer would get lost.

Thanks to Walta he spent a rather surreal twenty minutes on a planet that he was glad to see the back of. It possessed an exceptionally thin atmosphere, monotonous landscapes and very strange life forms. That any species should wish to spend vast amounts of effort and money to visit this overgrown rock proved very disconcerting to Slogg. And yet this appeared to be the precise aim of the inhabitants of his destiny planet.

Blupin Slingsling predicted the imminent arrival of the Earthman, complete with oxygen apparatus and someone called Ronald MacDonald.

"What must their own planet be like if they wish to get his one so much?" were Blupin's final words.

Slogg mused as he stared intently at the main screen, watching the little red planet disappear to an infinitesimal dot.

Walta, meanwhile, maintained that he had tried more than once to warn his Captain of the apparent lack of life-form, but upon the explicit order of *shut it* he had done so straight away. He maintained it proved fruitless to argue with his Captain and he had no intention of trying.

As the ship turned towards its new destination a weak star came into view.

Slogg ordered a brief pop into superluminal drive to speed their arrival on Earth. The stars on the screen turned to streaks as Walta obeyed his command silently. The sun grew bigger in size.

He turned to see Deluxia staring at him in a

thoughtful mood.

"How come," she said, "that if we travel faster than the speed of light, we can still see the stars shining?"

"It comes as part of your recruitment process," said Slogg.

"Oh yes?"

"Of course. We stipulate perfect eyesight and quick reactions," bluffed Slogg, who hadn't a clue.

"Well I never," sighed Deluxia, " I always believed it must be explained by the Very-Special Theory of Relativity, which states once an observer attains superluminal velocity they may see all light sources subtending an arc of less than one hundred and eighty degrees - although that source will be inversely compressed across the spectrum. The anomaly is rebalanced by the fact light is quantum in its nature. Relatively speaking that is."

There was a brief silence.

"Deluxia?" asked Slogg.

"Yes?"

"Have you ever considered applying for Captaincy?"

"No."

"Well please don't, because I'm perfectly happy as things are now."

The ship sped on and the stars in front remained visible. The Supercomputer told them of the Jegwurt Beasts of Ooklon Ten with a natural walking speed faster than light.

"The only way they found to slow down their lifestyle, and reduce the number of pavement deaths, was to invent a public transport system. Jegwurt Businessbeasts can now arrive late for meetings, walk a few paces, and reappear early!"

"Shut up!" said Slogg.

"Or you'll cut off my magnetic bubbles, I know."

Silence returned briefly to the bridge only to be broken by a report from Taroooc.

"The new planet is coming into range Sir."

"Is it *Earth*?"

"Yes Sir."

"Taroooc, are you sure?"

"Positive Captain. They're even putting out a beacon."

"A beacon. Well, how *civilised* of them. Is it a Galactic Core standard?"

"It's an attempt, Sir."

"They appear to know more than we gave them credit for. After our debacle on Mars maybe it's time I got the full story, and some pointers, from Dzkk. While I'm down that way I'll check on Clamburxer. I don't want him fouling things up."

"Aye, Sir."

"Are the cloaking shields still on?"

"Yes."

"Okay, let's keep it that way for now. We can't be too careful. Focus a cloaking tunnel on the beacon. Nothing outside of its channel sees us."

"Captain," called Walta, daring to speak again, "we've dropped from superluminal drive. Earth is coming into view."

"Okay good. It's basically just a job now, so let's get it over and done with."

Slogg was about to enter the lift when he stopped, his attention suddenly caught by the main screen. He stood and stared at it silently, as did the rest of his crew.

What had been a small pinpoint of light a few seconds earlier was now forming into a beautiful green and blue marble with wisps of white across its surface. Closer and closer, and with screen magnification on full, an intricate browns and oranges also became visible.

"Oh my. It really is beautiful," said Deluxia, "so delicate."

"That can't be natural. It looks like a promotion for Galactic Real Estate," observed Taroooc.

Slogg's thoughts were in the same vein. He had witnessed brightly mottled planets before, but none so subtle and exquisite. The planet exuded life - not forms yet visible in vast quantities - just *Life*.

"How could they give something so beautiful such an uninspiring name?" questioned Deluxia, "*Earth*!"

"We have a fix on the beacon Captain," reported Taroooc.

"Good."

Slogg continued to stare at the planet as it began to fill the screen.

"That is a truly awesome sight... and quite a destiny. I'm going to leave Clamburxer to his Jockey Monk beer. Deluxia please can you contact the *SPA* bay and ask Dzkk if he will join us on the bridge. He may wish to see this as well."

"Yes Sir."

"Tell him... we've arrived."

CHAPTER 34

Nelson's neck was aching, and he cupped his hand behind his head to support it.

"Have you never seen a sunrise before?" quipped Tina.

"Not through forty feet of rock! And never framed by three giant spines holding a massive chunk of Toblerone. I can't process it."

He had been transfixed for four minutes since the cavern roof turned non-existent. Three of these minutes were spent staring through the superstructure and on to a bright morning star which, apart from its own twinkling, remained clearly visible and had no allusion of fading as the sun slowly lit the sky.

"We appear to have achieved full stability," reported Charlie to his entourage of Knowalls, who were now in the business of returning to their touch screens or mobile devices.

A loud voice over the public address system broke Nelson's concentration with the sky.

"Beacon in operation. Imminent reply expected. We believe we have *them* located."

Beacon? Reply?

"Are *they… them*?" whispered Nelson confusingly to Charlie. Luckily the old man understood.

"Yes, Nelson, provided that we are talking of the same *them*."

"And this is *the meeting point*?" added Tina.

"Correct my dear."

"Extra-terrestrials?" hissed Nelson.

"*Yessss*!" hissed Charlie in mock subterfuge.

"Aliens? What on God's Earth am I looking at up there? And you all seem so casual. Such a low-key event. I was more excited than you, the last time I went to my

Uncle Brian's for tea."

"Well, we were all a little more excited… the first time that we made contact," admitted Charlie.

"The *first* time!" exclaimed Nelson, "You mean this isn't the first time that you've met."

"No, not exactly. The first time we didn't actually meet, we simply made contact. And a very strange sort of contact it was too."

"I feel another *explanation* coming on," sighed Tina.

"Always happy to help my dear."

"But I *want* to understand," exclaimed Nelson. "I need these explanations. This is momentous. I've dreamt about this… and making my own mountain of mashed potato."

Tina and Charlie both stared in disbelief at Nelson.

"Richard Dreyfus! No? Come on. *E.T…*"

"*Close Encounters* actually," corrected Tina, then she pleaded to Charlie, "Can we sit?"

"Of course."

He indicated a collection of high-backed stools arranged along one of the cavern's control consoles. Tina grabbed one and perched on it. Nelson gazed back at the needles, the Toblerone, his twinkling star and then decided to do the same. Charlie continued.

"So, have you heard of the Arecibo Message?"

"No," said Tina emphatically.

"Okay. In the early 70's one of our Progressionaries, Dre'8K over there…" Charlie indicated a bespectacled man with a white lab coat covering his navy-blue cardigan and matching tie, "…or Frank as we now call him, he proposed the idea of structured, extra-terrestrial communication. It was a logical step, but given the size of antenna we needed, and the difficulty in concealing it, Frank was keen to involve humanity. At a superficial level of course. A sort of, hiding in plain sight thing, like we do at NASA. Anyway, what you see, or don't see, here," said Charlie holding his hands skyward, "…the invisible dish, those towers, the suspended receiver, is what we built. The Arecibo Observatory…

"The what?" started Nelson.

"The largest reflector dish in the world, by an order of magnitude. It is carved into the Puerto Rican rock, and then bounces what it receives from outer space up to that steerable receiver, suspended on those cables."

"So, this is all a radar telescope and an observatory?"

"Yes Nelson, and this…" he extended an arm around, "is our *secret cave*. And finally, all of this doesn't just observe, it is also designed to *transmit*."

"Transmit."

"Yes, emit signals."

"To whom, aliens?"

"Yes, as it turns out… somewhat unexpectedly."

"*Really*! But why from Puerto Rico?"

"Well, our Frank here, and his unwitting human colleagues, designed the Arecibo Message to carry basic information about humanity and transmit it to the stars. To be honest it began more as a demo than a real attempt to start a conversation with ET.

"And ET phoned home?" jumped in Nelson.

"Not exactly. Our message was a simple series of coloured blocks depicting human form, numbers, atomic elements, you know, the boring stuff… sorry Frank. But then, a year ago we get back…

"Yes?"

"Well, a bit of UHD video…"

"UHD?" queried Nelson.

"*Ultra*-high definition… look, it doesn't matter. Luckily, humanity can't yet process UHD, but as Knowalls we were able to. So, Frank switches it to our private circuits and we see something that still seems a little hard to believe."

He paused to give added effect.

"Well?" asked Nelson, right on cue.

"Well… a clear moving image of… a giant egg."

"A *what*?"

"A giant egg. As clear as day, with the Andromeda galaxy right behind it."

"An egg?"

"It was the last thing we expected to see. So, the next day we go into a huddle in this very cave, and covertly send back our own bit of UHD. A few hours later our receiver issues a few pops and hisses, then all our lights go out, and a booming voice begins complaining about its lack of technical knowledge and Boom Etiquette. It then asked us who we were and what we were doing transmitting into that area of the Galaxy. We explained we were from Earth and the voice cried *Earth? Oh, crap…* and disappeared."

"Then what happened," asked Tina, as Charlie stopped to lick his lips and swallow.

"Well, weeks went by with us just listening. But one night the digital voice returned and started booming again. He announced himself as Desuck – we think - and said we had taken him completely by surprise. He told us to expect the arrival of a visiting party, if he could get the buy in and resources. And he said we should begin putting out another transmission beacon at this precise day and time. He also spoke of being all-powerful, which meant he couldn't explain too much because he hadn't taken the time to understand it himself. Then he disappeared again and the last thing we heard was a seemingly faulty electronic voice telling him to slow down. To which Desuck's voice replied *Shut it, Zero*. And that was, and is, it. Until now."

"That… is unbelievable," exclaimed Tina flatly.

"I understand. But I promise you, it's all true.

Another short silence ensued.

"Wait," said Nelson finally. "You are telling me

that the first contact between man and an alien life form is through an egg and a megaphone."

"I assure you Nelson, that is how it happened. You don't think we would take you and Tina through all this, only to tell you lies about the reason for it all."

"Maybe," said Nelson cynically, but he had little time to express any further doubt as the public address system interrupted them.

"The visitors are sighted and tracked, I repeat... ... er, what was it... oh yes, visitors sighted and tracked."

"There you go Nelson," concluded Charlie, "So I suggest you go back to staring skyward and let your eyes do the judging."

Charlie stepped forward as Nelson peered up expecting to see a giant egg, yet all he could see was the three-tower superstructure, a pale purple sky, a thin band of cloud, and his same star, which was now moving.

Moving.

In fact, it was moving and growing. And it was now a green and white star. And a pulsing red star. Then a blue and yellow one. And still it grew until it stopped being a collection of lights and became a collection of shapes that were joined by lights. And within these shapes there were other shapes, and more lights within these shapes... or possibly windows or portholes. And so, this was no weather balloon or unregistered military aircraft. This was an *ALIEN STARSHIP*.

But the closer it came the more Nelson worried. He was worried because the starship worried him. And the starship worried him because there something wrong with it. As it came closer, he worried more. This was no haute couture starship of the fantasy kind, or a mean looking black slab of the mysterious kind.

To Nelson it looked like a second-hand car of the unroadworthy kind. More accurately, it looked like a cruise-ship sized lollipop, spherical head and all, with three tail fins and a missing a dorsal. He was also sure that it just perceptibly wobbled as it approached.

Nelson sat on his high-backed stool in a secret cave, staring through the invisible rock and into the dawn sky at a looming alien starship.

Tina and Charlie were close by but deep in hushed conversation.

"So, you're quitting the Earth just as the aliens arrive?" stated Tina.

"Almost, but not quite," explained the Knowall. "We began thinking about reaching other solar systems around the same time as we put out the Arecibo Message. We realized this type of project needed masses more in terms of resources and funding. Hence Bill, Steve, the take-away coffee and all that bottled water. You need a lot of *bucks* to afford reaching the *stars*.

When we started planning it nearly 10 years ago, *The Quit* was always going to be what it states: quit the Earth. Leave humanity and its nuclear proliferation… to do what you will. We are off. But with our interplanetary technology we had reached about ten percent of light speed. To really quit, and reach a nice exoplanet, we need light speed… and beyond it."

"But that's impossible."

"It appears not. And we're nearly there. The theory is all sorted, we just need to get ourselves some *tachyons*."

"Some what?"

"It's all too complex Tina, honest. Young Bez'0S over there can explain it whenever you're ready."

Charlie indicated towards the youngest Knowall with the centre parting, who they met back in the Yorkshire bunker. He turned from his screen to smile at them and raise his strong eyebrows. Charlie continued.

"But the tachyons will help the spaceships Jeff is building travel faster than the speed of light. And to get them we need a *Large Hadron Collider*."

"I won't even ask…"

"Thank you, please don't. We've started that as well, underground as we do. But… it is going to cost billions. Megabucks. Star bucks."

He paused and held his hands skywards, taking in a deep breath.

"So, in summary, we were on a path to our light-speed rockets reaching the first chosen exoplanet. Then ET answered, and here we are. Hopefully they can show us the way!"

"Show you the way!" tuned in Nelson. "To where? *Taxi! Follow that alien…*" He was flummoxed and needed his VHS rewind button, or maybe better, a fast-forward.

Tina, on the other hand, was clear headed.

"So why are *we* here?" she asked.

"You two?"

"Yes. If you are eventually quitting the Earth faster than the speed of light, why do you need us two?"

"Nothing gets passed you does it," admired Charlie. "Well, we're not just building four-seater spaceships my dear. We're going to be building *arks*."

"Arks?"

"Yes, firstly because there's quite a few of us. And secondly, we'd like to take some of our friends with us to this new world… four legged and two legged."

"Hang on…" stuttered Nelson, "just a sec. So if I get this right, you're saying that you kidnapped us both to be lab rats on your interplanetary animal farm. Walking in, two by two."

Charlie turned to Nelson and sighed heavily.

"So harsh Nelson, such harsh words. You may remember you made the first move. We wanted to see what you knew and then offer you this opportunity. Tina was an unfortunate bystander, but now she can choose as well. You represent humanity. There will be other members of the animal kingdom selected as well. We want you to join us as equals. Hopefully, you will choose to once we are ready… because it's going to be quite an adventure!"

Nelson began processing. Again.

He eventually turned to Tina and spoke softly.

"Are you up for all of this?"

She smiled warmly back and reached her hand out to his shoulder and stroked it down his arm. She then turned back to Charlie.

"One more question," she said.

"Of course my dear. Please keep asking them."

As the starship approached, the cavern's occupants forgave it for being the wrong kind of hardware to engender a science fiction epic. It stopped wobbling and managed to defy gravity beautifully to glide slowly down without a hint of liquid fuelled engines. Contact had yet to be established and Charlie was content to leave it that way.

"Let them make the first move," he said.

"Can they see us down here?" asked Tina.

"Maybe not, but they will be most aware of our presence."

Nelson watched as the starship reined in its power and began a final manoeuvre. It was now clearly immense, and should it land directly on top of their cavern aperture, it would obliterate the dawn sky from view. However, it chose to halt slightly off-centre, leaving a third of the sky in view. Half the left flank of its central column and frontal sphere were lit by the rising sun. It did not land, but hovered just above two of the antenna towers, totally motionless, quiet, and with a variety of lights pulsing.

Nelson noticed the starship passed at least one criterion set down by earthborn film makers through the years. It had lots of twiddly bits underneath.

CHAPTER 35

The visiting craft was completely at rest. Its myriad of lights blinked leisurely and an eerie stillness crept across the whole vessel. Despite its dilapidated appearance the sheer size was enough to overwhelm the observer. Had Nelson known this was by no means the largest ship in the Galactic Core Fleet he would have been even more impressed. The ominous stillness continued from above, from the forest floor, and from the cavern below.

"What happens next?" Tina finally whispered.

"We can only wait and see. The ball is firmly planted in their court," replied Charlie.

Still the ship hung in the air with no visible means of support. And still it remained quiet.

"Aren't we supposed to play music to them or something?" suggested Nelson.

"Don't be so ridiculous," hissed Tina.

The silence stretched on and on. Nelson, Tina and the large collection of Knowalls waited for the first sign, the first glimpse, the first hint of an attempted communication between the two domains now represented. It was clear to all in the cavern that the aliens knew they were there.

Nelson imagined an undertaking of invisible scans across their primitive human bodies, soft probes into each delicate brain, and all without detection or challenge, to determine the optimum inter-species communication methodology. The cavern's inhabitants sensed they need only wait for their visitors to decide exactly how to commence this historic dialogue.

"Where *the hell* are they!" screamed Slogg to his crew.

"They must be around here somewhere Captain, the life-form detector confirms it, and it's never wrong," replied Taroooc.

"Have you ever tried it on yourself!" snarled Slogg. He frantically examined the main screen showing a quite remarkable sunrise highlighting an immense radio telescope dish seemingly cut out of solid rock, with dense forest all around, and a secluded airstrip in the middle distance. Significantly lacking from this view were any Earth people.

He looked back at Taroooc and hissed:

"Look at this. I risk bringing this ship right down to the planet's surface on some half-baked mission to create the biggest culture shock this species ever witnessed... and they just can't be bothered to turn up. Ha!"

Schtip.

The lift door opened and Dzkk stepped into bridge.

"And about time too! *Look.*"

Slogg held up both hands to indicate the main screen with its sunrise display.

"We are about to liberate a planet of nocturnal trees and a bowl of concrete."

"Patience Captain, patience. They are out there somewhere. Have you tried external communications?" suggested the old man.

"Patience. *Patience*! I'll give you patience. Patience is being about to qualify for three weeks leave on the Pleasure Planet of Pluvia, with its kinky mermaids and tired anglers, only to be stopped by a freak in an egg who wants to give four billion people a chance of getting to Pluvia first. That's patience! Of *course* we've tried external communications, haven't we Taroooc?"

"Er…"

"Taroooc!"

"No, sorry Captain."

Slogg returned to his chair and slumped deeply into it.

Yet again Taroooc managed to drain every ounce of energy from Slogg's weary body. He rested an elbow on the armrest and propped his head by sinking his fist firmly into his right cheek.

"Okay Taroooc, let's try external communications."

All was very quiet in the cavern. Then came sudden, immediate shock and alarm. Switching on external communications initiated a large transient spike across the hovering starship's peripheral speakers. This produced an extremely loud and reverberant boom, followed by hissing and crackling. Then:

"... eople ... f Earth, we brin… greetin… rom the …alactic C... and welc… y… to our Federa… … …

… don't …ink that thi… micropho… is working. *Tap tap thump*."

Then, only rumblings, as a none too well disguised struggle ensued for possession of the faulty microphone.

In the cavern they politely listened and waited.

Finally:

"….ive that to me! Captain Deutronimus Karben Slogg here. We before you represent the Galactic Core Fleet of Starships and have been sent to Earth with the express instructions to inf… you th… ur ...ing. But w... k... ...in thi… op… …ry. Damn this f… ing equipment. *Bang. BANG!* ...esting testi… one two thr... f…r. Could w... please have someone l…k at this. *BANG!*."

A short pause followed, then three clicks.

"… now? Sure? Okay, let's try again. I repeat, my name is Captain Slogg, and I come here to representing Galactic Core Fleet. We are here to welcome you into the Galactic Club. I am lucky to have with me aboard one of the universe's masters, known to us all as Dzkk. Together we would very much like to meet you and commence talks on a variety of topics, not least of which is your contribution to the Galactic Community Budget. But first things first.

Where are you?"

As this unfolded Charlie requested a simpler two-way contact link be established from the cavern to bypass the laser multiplied sonic resonators and narrowband echo beams designed in anticipation of their visitors advanced communication methods.

Consequently, all the exits leading from their cavern to ground level were opened, and Charlie used the public address at full volume to yell:

"*We're down here!*"

Then a pause.

"*Dzzmmmm…* Well could you come up where we can see you," came the reply, "We'd be most grateful."

Slogg held the microphone horizontally at arm's length and let it drop to the floor. He prepared a cold stare and Taroooc winced.

Meanwhile Deluxia smiled and offered a piece of information Slogg had no wish to receive at this point in time.

"Apologies Captain, but reports are coming in of a rather drunken Chief Commissioner Clamburxer careering around the lower decks with a very large pink elephant in tow."

"Deluxia! Did I really *need* that information right now? Have Security contain them and, if necessary, I give permission to sedate the elephant and shoot Clamburxer."

"Yes Captain. Oh, and Captain."

"Yes?"

"Look up there! It appears one of their doorways has just lit up... on, on the corner of the screen. They are about to show themselves!"

On the main screen they saw an exit at the edge of the airstrip, already opened to assist speaker-to-speaker communication, now display a brilliantly lit interior contrasting sharply with its dark surroundings. Mysterious shapes began to coalesce from within.

"I always thought it was our job to do this to them," exclaimed Slogg watching the strange shapes form into moving creatures as they emerged into the open air.

"I wonder what they look like?" said Deluxia.

"They're probably green with pointy ears," guessed Taroooc. Behind him Walta self-consciously touched each tip of his.

Ten or more Earthling figures became clearer as they neared the starship. Anticipation on Slogg's face disappeared with sudden recognition.

"Well, that's boring," he said, "they look exactly the same as us. Within reason."

"Such is *Life*," observed Dzkk.

They watched as the Earthlings delicately approached the starship with trepidation. They came close, but very wary to be completely beneath its huge mass.

"Well... let the show begin. Lower the underside hatch Taroooc, and then join me and Dzkk down there," ordered Slogg as he walked to the lift.

Taroooc flipped switches, announced the hatch was opening, and joined the others in the lift as Slogg closed the doors.

Deep below them, a faint rumbling was audible as the largest access hatch located on the underbelly of the ship began its slow, laborious swing open.

Nelson watched stupefied from the reverse side, as the slow opening offered a darkened entrance into the mysterious starship. Only seconds earlier he registered the aliens had been talking to him in English, having initially accepted it without thought. Only now did he question the dubious nature of this. The starship's belly was opening, and Nelson decided to ask for an explanation at the nearest opportunity.

The hatch came to a halt two feet above the ground, forming a gently curved ramp that led to another world. Briefly a light flickered inside, and three pairs of rather ordinary legs appeared at the top of this makeshift stairway.

Two wore trousers, the other appeared to be wrapped in a feather trimmed cloak framing strange yellow boots that highlighted four toes on each foot.

"Well, they are bipedal – that bit looks like us," commented Charlie to Emm, Dex and all those around him who were similarly bending down, curious to examine the top half of the aliens' bodies.

"And so… does the rest of us," echoed Slogg walking down the ramp with Dzkk and Taroooc in tow. "A little boring isn't it, apart from a few skin tones, the odd poultry reference, and Tarooоc's third eye… but you'll get used to those. Please don't bother to peek, it would seem that over half the universe has evolved into the well tried and tested model that makes us mostly humanoid. And Eustachian tube implants help us all speak the same language. So…"

He then took a sharp intake of breath and took a very lengthy pause.

A sense of panic swept through Slogg's whole body. His mind went blank. It followed the dawning realisation he never penned or practiced an opening speech. He had been presented with a destiny, yet no one had prepared him for what to say or do on this momentous occasion.

How would it go down in history?

He flashed a look at Dzkk, and the old man simply smiled back at him in wide-eyed expectation. Likewise, these Earth people were hanging on his every word. This unplanned dramatic pause was building tension further. His mind raced back in time to his Astronomical Academy tutor Fid Fadood, and his Classics lecture option *23 Immutable Laws to Make Yourself Likeable in Command*. Fadood's unique advice on addressing any new multi-species audience included the memorable phrase *patter and banter*.

He quickly decided his best tactic, his only tactic. *Patter and banter.* He pressed on:

"So… we're here to welcome you into the Galactic Club, and it appears you are forty annums early. Well, you know what they say… time flies like an arrow, fruit flies like a banana."

He hoped this ice-breaker might do the trick, but there were blank, puzzled faces across all these Earthly companions. Slogg panicked. He was already losing his new audience.

"Anyway, hello!" he brazened, "My name is Captain Slogg and this is my Biophysics Officer Taroooc. And this… is a master of the universe, Dzkk."

"Hello," began Charlie, "my name is…"

Slogg's patter somehow slipped into overdrive.

"Good, good. We have come to liberate your planet from its primitive trappings and introduce you to the constant upgrades of intergalactic technology: flying eggs; Occasional Kill Weapons; TwiText and Instagran; Ireen Y'Know What Ah Mean; Teleport Stream gender reassignment; the list is endless."

Charlie coughed lightly, the internationally accepted sign that you politely wish to be given chance talk. International, but perhaps not universal.

Slogg ploughed on. "Yes, galactic scientific achievements... which brings us to my ship. It is ready to whisk a few of your *human race* away, to witness the wonders of the universe. And there will be other ships bringing some of the universe's interesting life-forms to your doorstep. Life-forms such as the Dinglydanglers from the planet Dongle... lovely people to hang out with," and he winked at his audience.

Charlie took his chance.

"But that's just it," he began, "you see the rest of the human race don't..."

"Of course... *don't* want to miss out! And they won't, no need to worry," continued Slogg. "Everything has been taken care of, hasn't it Dzkk?"

"Hmm?"

"There you are you see, your worries are unsubstantiated. After all, I'm sure we've dealt with bigger planets than this. I mean, you're not exactly monstrous or supremely huge - just middling to cute. But we can sort that out when necessary. Planet enlarging is big Geltoes these days."

The verbal outflow just continued as his adrenalin flowed.

"Mind you, don't get me wrong, four billion people isn't so small either, especially when all your transport vehicles, visual display screens, and toothbrushes have to be licensed. A lot of digitizing. But I digress. So… where are the rest of your four billion friends?"

"Well, that's what I've been trying to tell you," said Charlie, "You see, we don't exactly represent the human race, we..."

"But of course you do!" assured Slogg, "I think you've got hold of the wrong end of the laser-pointer there…"

He was *off script*, yet there was no script for him to be on.

"We haven't come down to this planet to meet some second-rate dignitaries with *World Leader* stamped in their forehead. Give them half a chance and they'll fluff the whole thing up. No, we've come to meet the real people - the people like you with the robes and the braiding. The none too clever, the none too ambitious, the none too obnoxious. The little people without whom there would be no planet, no Earthlings. That's who we've come to meet."

There was a long moment of silence, eventually broken by an extremely loud and very confused exclamation.

"*Toothbrushes!*" Nelson found himself shrieking.

"I'm sorry?" queried Slogg.

"You just said that all toothbrushes have to be licensed in the universe."

"Why of course. Is that not normal here?"

Slogg returned to overdrive. His pace increased.

"They have to be regularly checked for weakening strength and structure. Dental hygiene is of extreme importance to the modern interstellar traveller, particularly on public transport. In the eastern spiral arm of your own Milky Way one can be arrested for possessing bad breath and charged with polluting the atmosphere. It's only natural."

At this point Dzkk raised his eyes and pointed nose to the brightening sky and gave a deep sigh. With his face portraying the fatigue of infinite wisdom he wrapped his feather cloak tight around his body and turned slowly to walk back up the ramp. A heavy burden was beginning to press down on his shoulders again.

Slogg observed his departure.

"The poor man needs rest. It's beginning to take its toll. It's alright Dzkk, I'll take care of things down here," he shouted after him.

Dzkk shook his head softly from side to side.

Charlie opened his mouth to explain the difference between Nelson, Tina, his colleagues and the reason they were together. But he was not quick enough.

Patter and banter. Fadood's advice drove Slogg ever onwards.

"As Captain of the ship above I will of course invite you to partake in a light meal at my table to enjoy the universal delights of micro-grilled staphylococci in a rich agar sauce. And as for our chef, bless his heart… before you *eat it*!"

No response and Slogg was sweating. A new fear was emerging, *The Fear of Empty Time*, and bad jokes were not helping.

Charlie came to his rescue.

"Listen!" he exclaimed, trying desperately to assert himself, "Will you let me explain. You see, Nelson and Tina here are different from the rest of us. They represent the true cold-blooded human race who have wars and things. Wars with bloodshed over petty, stupid arguments. While the rest of us are… well, we're…"

'Vegetarians?" interrupted Slogg, "well not to worry, we can fry up some petals from the talking flowers of Segazoa, or the odd root from the walking sugar beet of Pendrianu Five. No problem."

Dzkk was now at the top of the ramp and turned to give a final look towards Slogg, Taroooc and the Earthlings. He made every effort not to sigh, but he could not hold it in.

With a small shrug of the shoulders, he was about

to re-enter the starship when he became acutely aware of a strong smell of alcohol and sensed the floor shuddering beneath his feet.

One glimpse was all he needed to discern the horrendous shape of Chief Commissioner Milko Clamburxer pounding along the corridor towards the hatchway, followed by an equally horrific, doubly inebriated, pink elephant. The shock of this made Dzkk reel, which was all that saved him by a hair's breadth from being trampled underfoot. The wretched beast stampeded past with the huge flailing ears, and pink trunk waving side to side.

Ahead of it Clamburxer yelled something resembling *Charge!* and flew on down the ramp into the early morning light of Earth.

"Oh crap!" yelled Taroooc as he caught sight of the monstrosity hurtling towards him. Whereas Slogg, not blessed with an eye in the back of his head, was slower to react.

As luck had it, though Slogg would disagree profusely at the time, he was hit first by the full force of the crazed Clamburxer and together they performed a twisted ballet of mangled bodies and beer fumes. They flew through the air in surreal slow-motion, crash landed in a crumpled mess, then rolled a few more feet, entwining with dried grass and soil. In a contorted heap, they came to a dusty halt at Tina's feet.

The elephant, meanwhile, following close behind, trumpeted supremely in sheer admiration of this spectacle. On hitting the bottom of the ramp, it went into an uncontrollable skid on the dry soil and span a full one hundred and eighty degrees, finally settling in a cloud of dust on very wobbly legs, with a dazed, possessed look in its eyes.

Everyone else remained stock still and totally silent.

Clamburxer was the first to open his dirt

encrusted eyes and look up. What he saw caused him to blink twice.

"Cor! Jush look up th... them legs," he stammered as Tina stepped backwards away from his lecherous glare.

"I think I'd b... *hic* better arresht myself ..."

Slogg opened his eyes, and they widened in horror. As the dust cleared, he discerned the rather large behind of the poor, inebriated elephant. Its tail and buttocks were twitching. He had no idea the effect Braevitchkan beer may have on an animal's digestive system. He watched the elephant's knees tremble and then wobble, as its large rear end appeared ever more unsettled.

And so, with far more speed and dexterity than his state would normally allow, Slogg became free of Clamburxer, got to his feet and stepped aside. Clamburxer tried many times to raise himself from the ground but failed miserably.

He lifted his head, his helmet finally fell off, and through squinting eyes said:

"This is a raid. Take all your cl... *hic* wh, where *hic* am I?"

"Who is this *tramp*?" Tina asked disgustedly.

"Ah, this is Chief Commissioner Clamburxer. He's in charge of policing your sector of the universe."

"And that?" continued Tina, indicating the huge, quivering monstrosity beside Slogg.

"Er, that… is a pink elephant."

The beast finally emptied its bowels.

From somewhere deep within the starship Dzkk groaned and decided that it was time to lie down. Below him maintenance crews and robots had finally emerged from the ship to supervise, with some difficulty, the coaxing of their now bewildered elephantine beast back inside.

Clamburxer tried desperately to assert his authority with a refusal to re-enter the ship. However, the task of standing proved so intensely complicated he eventually succumbed to a robotic stretcher and was carried back aboard.

Slogg sent for the cleaning droids.

CHAPTER 36

"So," began Slogg, as a droid polished his left cheek with a warm towel, "can we have a few of you on board for a preliminary trip, before the rest of the universe arrives? There's no time to waste you know."

Each of the Knowalls turned slowly to Charlie, eyeing him anxiously. Before them, the whole universe beckoned, offering unrestricted experience of its riches. Yet no one had been selected to go first. Assuming their own development of a tachyon drive would propel the Knowall's new ships into the cosmos, they had yet to choose who would take the first step.

Charlie stared at Slogg for a short while, summing the very recent events in his mind. It was up to him to make the decision now and he had to be careful. His eyes broke contact with Slogg's and he began a long, slow scan of his fellow Knowalls and their two friends. Tina fixed him with a stern face. Nelson smiled limply.

Although Charlie appeared to be appraising his companions, he was not seeing them. His mental cogs were in frantic motion, churning ideas and repercussions. The same decision kept choking up, trying to be reversed, but it was vital and strong from the mighty forces that drove it.

With final recognition of the eager anticipation showing on his colleagues faces, Charlie looked into the glacier blue eyes of his most trusted colleague, Emm'8k. Steadfast and unmoving, she stared straight back for a few seconds and there was the minutest shake of her head. Charlie smiled and let his decision be known.

"No," he said.

"No?"

"No."

"I... I'm sorry?" stuttered Slogg.

"No, you can't have a few of us aboard."

"But…"

"In fact, you can't have any of us aboard. And we would appreciate it if you would ask the rest of the universe not to visit us for a good while yet. Please."

"Bu… but… but you can't do that. No one can say *no*. There must be… But no one refuses, do they Dzkk?"

But Dzkk was lying down in a darkened waiting room of the *SPA* bay. He had foreseen this outcome and had no intention of witnessing the final humiliation.

Slogg's palms began to sweat and then itch. He stared at Charlie and then looked frantically around the rest of the Knowalls. Each of their faces portrayed a similar feeling - one of relief. They were all thankful not to have been picked to go first.

"This is ridiculous. You… you… whatever you call yourself," spat Slogg.

"The name is Charlie, and I've grown to like it. Charles Arthur Clarke. And Charles Arthur Clarke is staying on Earth for a good time to come. It may be nowhere near perfect here, but it's a damn sight better than…" and then he stopped in a sudden show of tact.

"Well, let's just say that I could imagine worse. And if *all* the human race can't sort out its problems then bang goes this *cute* little planet, as you so delicately put it. So, I think, maybe it's about time we got back together with humanity and tried to help our fellow *Earthlings*, rather than opting out. You never know, it just might be possible to make some sense out of it together."

"I'm confused. I thought that you were all part of the human race?" quieried Slogg, baffled further.

"Yes! You are *exactly* right there, Captain. And I think it's something that we've all forgotten. And as far as the nuclear threat goes, and the Cold War of East versus West… well my dear colleague Mikhail Gee has been espousing some ideas. It's clear we should be listening to more. The Gee is short for Gorbachev by the way."

"Spasibo Comrade Charles. Thank you," said one of the shorter Knowalls in a strong Russian accent. Slogg noticed a strange red mark on the man's forehead.

"You are welcome Mikhail. Let's talk more about your Perestroika idea. Maybe now is the time for you to implement this *surface* plan."

"Da Tovarishch Clark. Is good for me."

Charlie looked around his fellow group of Knowalls. The young Fry smiled back at him and whispered profoundly:

"It only takes a spaceship full of aliens for the Knowalls and Humanity to realise how much we have in common."

"Indeed," hushed Charlie, "Good quote, keep that one."

He then raised his voice and said much louder: "So, it's decided. We are staying put."

There was a long pause.

"What… are… you… *talking about*!" yelled Slogg in disbelief. "East, West, Gorba someone, surface, staying put… it makes no sense! No one stays put."

"Well, we are."

"Are you sure?" said Slogg, slowly finding himself at a loss for *patter and banter*.

Charlie glanced around and there was a general nodding of agreement from the Knowalls.

"Can I ask you to reconsider," started Slogg. "You see, this is my destiny. I was chosen to bring you in. The powers that be will not be very impressed with me."

"I'm really sorry, but it seems like we have all made up our minds," said Charlie. "In retrospect we probably should have talked a little more between ourselves before setting off that beacon to bring you down here. I guess we all got a little over-excited – but now we *know* we are making the right decision."

"Ha! Unbelievable. Well, I guess that's it," sighed Slogg. "Mission accomplished you might say… *Not*."

"I guess we should apologise for contacting you in the first place," smiled Charlie.

"Perhaps we could try again sometime?"

"Perhaps."

"I don't suppose you'd like a nice pink elephant as a Peacefulness and Primacy Offering?"

"A what?"

"And we brought some beer too."

"No thank you," said, Charlie politely.

"Are you sure?"

There was no answer to Slogg's question, just a firm stare and a very slight shrug of the shoulders.

"That's it then? So, I think we'd better be off," he looked at the floor for a few second, then looked up again.

"Which way is the North Star?"

"The pub or the astronomical reference?"

"Both would be good, but I meant the latter," sighed Slogg.

"That way," said Charlie, pointing into the morning sky. "You'll see it clearly once you get above the atmosphere."

"Actually..." began Slogg, having just thought of a new angle on which he could approach this situation.

But the look on the Knowall's face said it all. He also knew deep inside himself that something had gone very, very wrong. He would probably spend the next few days and sleepless nights analyzing what just happened, running it through his brain repeatedly.

He turned and walked dejectedly up the ramp and back into his ship. He was now suffering from a severe case of the Big Bang Blues[25].

---

[25] This is the appropriate term for the condition in which any mortal may find themself when bringing into question their own existence, and what it equates to on the scale of a near infinite universe.

"Is that all Sir?" asked Taroooc as he passed.

"It would seem so," sighed Slogg, "As you come up, please would you close the hatch?"

"Yes, Captain."

"Ah yes, that's better" sighed Slogg, "*Captain…*"

Slogg and Taroooc stood at the top of the ramp and watched the Earthlings with a sense of loss. The hatch was rising slowly and Slogg started to play the events through his mind, imagining how his failings would be explained to him at great length during the mission debrief.

He exhaled heavily whilst the doorway gears completed their motion to shut out the Earth's daylight.

Suddenly from below they both heard one of the Earthling's distant voices.

"Wait a minute!" shouted Nelson with the hatch a few seconds from closing.

"Can I come?"

EPILOGUE

It is not in the stars to hold our destiny but in ourselves.
1599, William Shakespeare

3rd September
12:00noon AST, Puerto Rico

A single face peered from a scratched, dimly lit portal as the huge starship prepared to leave a planet it had visited only briefly.

The eyes gazed down at a collection of similar faces staring straight back, portraying feelings that ranged between resignation and bewilderment. Just one face below held tears in its eyes.

It was the same face that begged Nelson not to join the aliens, much to his own surprise. However, he convinced both himself and the face's owner this was the best thing for him, and he was categorical nothing could convince him otherwise.

Only now was he having the slightest twinge of regret regarding his decision.

But it was too late.

The invisible force that held the starship motionless above the ground was reshaping to smoothly lift its huge bulk from the Earth's gravitational pull.

Nelson watched as this massive power raised them slowly skyward, producing shockwaves that whipped up the dust and fallen leaves below. These forces became so great they threatened to overturn anyone or anything too close outside.

The tearful face was keeping a safe distance, but she still had to hold on tightly to her raincoat.

At long last the ship began to turn, screaming its low-flight Subtachyon engines at the ground directly beneath.

Disconsolately the tearful face spontaneously raised a hand to wave goodbye and blow a kiss. The fingers on the other hand also wiped the gusted grit from her eye. But her timing was poor as the immense forces needed for the lift off suddenly propelled open her unprotected raincoat, to reveal exactly what Tina was wearing underneath.

Nelson left the porthole and stayed no longer to watch.

Just seventeen seconds later he was in the starship's bridge, asking if it was possible to be put back down on the ground.

Printed in Great Britain
by Amazon